A CHRISTMAS CAROL

A CHRISTMAS CAROL

By

Jay Dubya

www.bookstandpublishing.com

[TBS]_1

Cover art and design by Al Margolis

ISBN [TBS]

Dedicated in memory of Charles Dickens

Other Books by Jay Dubya

Adult Fiction

Black Leather and Blue Denim, A '50s Novel
The Great Teen Fruit War, A 1960' Novel
Ron Coyote, Man of La Mangia
Frat' Brats, A '60s Novel
Pieces of Eight
Pieces of Eight, Part II
Pieces of Eight, Part III
Pieces of Eight, Part IV
The Wholly Book of Genesis
The Wholly Book of Exodus
The Wholly Book of Doo-Doo-Rot-on-Me
Thirteen Sick Tasteless Classics
Thirteen Sick Tasteless Classics, Part II
Thirteen Sick Tasteless Classics, Part III
Thirteen Sick Tasteless Classics, Part IV
Thirteen Sick Tasteless Classics, Part V
So Ya' Wanna' Be A Teacher!
Mauled Maimed Mangled Mutilated Mythology
Fractured Frazzled Folk Fables & Fairy Farces
FFFF & FF, Part II
Nine New Novellas
Nine New Novellas, Part II
Nine New Novellas, Part III
Nine New Novellas, Part IV
One Baker's Dozen
Two Baker's Dozen
RAM: Random Articles and Manuscripts
Time Travel Tales
Modern Mythology
UFO: Utterly Fantastic Occurrences
Prime-Time Crime Time
Snake Eyes and Boxcars
Snake Eyes and Boxcars, Part II
The Psychic Dimension
The Psychic Dimension, Part II
Shakespeare: Slammed, Smeared, Savaged and Slaughtered
Shakespeare: S, S, S & S, Part II
First Person Stories
The Arcane Arcade

vi

Thirteen Tantalizing Tales
PLOTS
PLOTS, Part II
THEMES
Hawthorne: Hacked, Shakespeare: Sacked, & Thurber: Thwacked
Hawthorne: Hazed, Hooked, Hammered and Hijacked
Suite 16
The FBI Inspector
Poe: Pelted, Pounded, Pummeled and Pulverized
Twain: Tattered, Trounced, Tortured and Traumatized
London: Lashed, Lacerated, Lampooned and Lambasted
O. Henry: Obscenely and Outrageously Obliterated
Homer's Odd Sea Odyssey
HOMER'S ILL ILIAD
Homer's Ill Iliad and Odd Sea Odyssey
The Timeless Time Machine
War of the Worlds
The Invisible Man
Parody Paradise
Parody Paradise, Part II
Parody Paradise, Part III
Parody Paradise, Part IV

Young Adult Fantasy Novels and Stories

Pot of Gold
Enchanta
Space Bugs, Earth Invasion
The Eighteen Story Gingerbread House

Introduction

Charles Dickens (1812-1870) spent most of his life in London and hadn't the foggiest notion why the hell he had ever done so. Dickens had a horrible childhood. His father had financial debts, so the government gave young Charles "the dickens" by making his father live in poorhouses and workhouses, but fortunately, not reside inside any popular government whorehouses. Dickens' terrible exposure to poverty later made him a literary crusader advocating for social justice. Such novels as *David Copperfield* and *Oliver Twist* truly reflect Charles Dickens's tremendous empathy for impoverished urban British children, along with their exploitation by the snobbish, unsympathetic, and apathetic adult industrial world.

Later in life, Dickens edited a magazine; was an amateur thespian, but the writer was not known to frequently associate with professional lesbians. The quite distinguished author gave many readings of his works throughout Europe, and even did so while touring slums in the United States. The British literary giant was a contemporary of the great Mark Twain, and the two eminent men did meet, although Dickens was much older during the height of *their* dual fames.

Some of Charles Dickens' famous novels are *A Tale of Two Cities, Great Expectations,* and *The Pickwick Papers*. One of his most popular short-fiction works had first been published in 1843 and was titled "A Christmas Carol", which featured a great character transformation in the personality of Ebenezer Scrooge from an old curmudgeon to a kind and loving benefactor. The story had been written in four sections known as "Staves", and herein is a parody re-write of "A Christmas Carol."

A Christmas Carol is Jay Dubya's 69th published book. Besides Adult Satire, the prolific author writes in seven other separate genres being: Action/Adventure Novels, Non-Fiction Books, Mythology, Science-Fiction, Detective Stories, Paranormal Short Stories, and Young Adult Fantasy Novels.

Contents

Stave One: "Jacob Marley's Ghost" 1

Stave Two: "The First of the Three Spirits" 43

Stave Three: "The Second of the Three Spirits" 75

Stave Four: "The Last of the Three Spirits" 105

Stave One
"Jacob Marley's Ghost"

Jacob Marley was dead, and there was no doubt that the old skinflint rightly deserved the inevitable fate. The stingy bastard's death certificate had been signed by the minister, by the government clerk, by the undertaker, by a Cockney pimp, by three disgusting, ugly harlots, and by Ebenezer Scrooge, who was Marley's chief mourner. And Scrooge had good credit all over London, but the parsimonious, hoary narcissist pinched every halfpenny in his pocket, and meticulously had polished every farthing inside his house's safe. Scrooge was a selfish, cheap, frugal bastard, and had been almost twice as covetous as Jacob Marley had been, no doubt about it.

Old Marley was as dead as King Tut's disintegrated scrotum. Scrooge logically knew that the miserable curmudgeon was truly dead, but the heartless partner believed that such a macabre fate would never hostilely descend upon himself.

'Marley and I had been business partners and devout capitalists for decadent decades,' Ebenezer thought and ruminated. 'And I was his sole executor; his sole administrator; his sole legal representative; his sole confidante; his sole mentor, his sole tormentor, and his sole mourner, who, for the permanent record, my remorseless, passionless heart did not officially or extensively mourn one iota for the no-good bastard.'

Scrooge was actually too cheap to paint-out Marley's name that appeared in the forty-year-old shingle above the door outside their import-export trading firm. *Scrooge and Marley*, the lackluster sign read, and in small letters below had been printed *Imports, Exports and Jamaican Reggae Music.* Some new customers called Scrooge "Scrooge", and other newcomers called Scrooge "Marley". Ebenezer automatically answered to either name because for many years, the miser and

Jacob Marley had been like one incomparable, cheapskate spirit.

Scrooge was a tightfisted, covetous, cantankerous, wrenching, scraping, clutching, avaricious old sinner. The arrogant fuck didn't know or care about the difference between summer heat and winter frost. He was much more bitter than any nasty January wind that ever gusted upon London. In fact, those January winds were the only blow-jobs that Scrooge ever received. Foul weather was the man's loyal ally and welcomed companion. According to Ebenezer Scrooge, little things such as the weather and the time of day were discussions that only the mediocre working class should value and find worthy of discussing while actively engaging in trite conversation. Money and business were the only damned relevant topics that captured Ebenezer Scrooge's pathetic, microscopic imagination, or concerned the man's damned narrow range of monetary interests.

Nobody ever stopped Scrooge in the street and stated with felicity, "My dear Scrooge, how the hell are ya'?" No beggars, monkey organ grinders, or desperate hookers ever solicited his attention. No curious children ever dared asking Scrooge what time of day it was, or how long or short his dick was. No man or woman ever asked the obvious social isolate directions to a store, to a church, to a mosque, to a cemetery, or to an Al Qaeda camp. Even the blind man's dog would tug its owner in the opposite direction when the alert animal noticed the tight weasel strolling towards them with *his* head crestfallen. Canines saved their barks and cats their meows for more threatening human dangers than to fruitlessly waste *their* limited time and energy upon the despicable, greedy, cold-hearted codger.

But Scrooge didn't give two flying farts about what others thought and gossiped. Ebenezer was the center of the universe as far as his ego considered, and everyone else was worthless space junk floating around *his* magnificent existence. The ingrate's total being seemed to radiate a subtle negative signal to all those pathetic humans that cluttered his path and got in his way. The unverbalized transmission seemed to say, 'Get out of my goddamned path, assholes, and keep your piss-head bullshit to yourselves, you stupid-shit fools!'

Yes, human sympathy and emotion had to keep its distance as the robotic, stone-hearted aged wretch daily trekked an almost perfect triangle from his poorly furnished apartment, to the marble pillared Trade Exchange, and then to his shabby accounting house office.

* * * * * * * * * * * *

Once upon a time, during an ordinary Christmas Eve, old Scrooge sat like a miserable miser inside his sterile-atmosphere counting house, wondering why such a thing as a plain Christian holiday could make so many stupid, debt-stricken workingmen and their abject-poverty families be filled with good cheer, along with the simple joy of gift giving. It was a frigid, bleak afternoon, and

London's clocks and church bells (the ones that were working) had just struck three, but it was already quite dark out, being only several frigid days after the gloomy winter solstice.

Scrooge kept the door inside his office open, so that the cheap bastard could maintain a distrustful surveillance upon his blithe clerk, Bob Crotchit, who sat in a sort of sunken tank, always looking like he was taking a bath, or enjoying a good shit while diligently copying pertinent business letters. Ebenezer Scrooge maintained a tiny fire but, Crotchit's fire was even quite smaller, so that the employer could economize and rather fanatically practice his extreme frugality at his clerk's expense.

'I'm allowed only one coal at a time to stay warm,' Bob quite sadly thought. 'Now, it's a whopping forty-five degrees inside my work tank, and that's with my two flimsy candles burning close to my face.'

Wily Ebenezer Scrooge kept the main coal box stocked inside *his* off-limits small office, and possessively guarded the fuel treasure against being raided. Every time Crotchit would come in to beg for an additional small coal to incinerate, old Scrooge would chew *his* ass out, and make poor Bob feel like a piece of sewer crap. "Wear your moth-infested, winter comforter, Robert Crotchit!" Scrooge lustily bellowed. "And occasionally, rub your hands together to cause friction and heat. But don't do it too often, or else you'll have to stay an additional hour to make-up the work you've lost while scraping your goddamned palms together!"

"Uncle, a Merry Christmas to you!" yelled Scrooge's nephew Fred as the aged coot's key employee jovially entered the counting house. The happy heir-to-be of *Scrooge and Marley* had startled his uncle with his boisterous "nonsensical flagrant cheerfulness".

"Bah, humbug!" Scrooge exclaimed as the mercurial, contemptible mogul involuntarily uttered the peculiar name of a local London exterminating company. "Yes. Bah humbug, I said!"

"Christmas, a humbug, you say, Uncle!" Fred hardily laughed. "I'm sure you don't mean what you've opined. That's just like insisting that happiness is a vile curse, and that good humor is a harmful pestilence!"

"Humbug, Fred! Humbug, I insist!" Scrooge boomed, almost as loud as a military cannon. "Screw Christmas! You and other assholes like yourself don't realize that Christmas screws you really good, right up the ass every December 25th. You habitually buy expensive, impractical toys along with exorbitant gifts for family and acquaintances, of which you really can't afford! Just look at unimportant Crotchit sitting over there," the caustic old proprietor indicated. "Bob already has a large, fucked-up family that the chap can't afford to keep. If Crotchit were smart, he would've learned to keep his dick inside his tattered pants, and only use his organ to take a piss now and then."

"But Uncle Scrooge," Fred merrily returned. "Christmas season has its basis as a sacred time of the year in which to rejoice for our blessings, and to venerate the Almighty. It's a good, charitable time for people to mingle and to celebrate each other's joyful company," the euphoric nephew suavely elaborated. "Men and women generally seem to be in wonderful agrecment during this special season, and we all realize we're merely pilgrims journeying on a mutual procession to the graveyard, and no one is really any better than the other, be they rich or be they poor!"

"Total nonsense and poppycock!" Ebenezer angrily argued. "Christmas finds most people, and you included, Nephew, as being a year older, but not a minute wealthier. And then moronic assholes like yourself tack on additional frivolous expenses to aggravate your economic plight, and in the process, sending your wealth spiraling-down towards bankruptcy. Any gay or straight shit-head that goes around the streets proclaiming 'Merry Christmas!' to his fellow doltish British-men ought to be burned to death in boiling pudding, and subsequently buried with a stake of holly hammered through his or her heart! Yes, the gay idiot should!"

"Uncle! That utterly preposterous comment is totally sacrilegious and being borderline blasphemous!" Fred answered in a shocked tone of voice. "Your excessive, deplorable sarcasm is indeed most unwarranted, and most unappreciated."

"Nephew, you keep Christmas in your own damned way, and kindly reciprocate by allowing me to keep the useless holiday in mine!" Scrooge lividly retorted. "Christmas is a silly, poor man's celebration that keeps stupid, garrulous, obnoxious shits like *you* poor, and then cleverly makes them even poorer!"

"Keep it, Uncle! But *you* fail to keep it!" Fred obstinately maintained. "In fact, I dare say, you've never kept it!"

"Well then, argumentative Nephew, leave it alone, and also leave me *alone,* because I don't need *a loan*, unlike you and Bob Cratchit," Scrooge rankled and joked as best as he could. "Much good this winter holiday has ever profited you, you harebrained, pencil-necked imbecile!"

"Uncle, there is in this world spiritual comfort, in addition to material comfort and monetary reward," Fred rationally insisted. "And although Christmas has never put a gold sovereign into my pocket, I believe it has done me spiritual good, and that it'll continue to bless me. So, I say, God bless it!"

Bob Crotchit (who was not taking a dump as it appeared from Scrooge's office) had been eavesdropping on the heated conversation, and the clerk tacitly applauded Fred's noble oratory. Ebenezer gave Bob such a penetrating stare and facial frown that the industrious-but-intimidated, underpaid fellow put his head to his chest, and pretended to be jotting-down his endless statistics. But Bob still was listening to the mild argument occurring in the adjoining office, as anxious Crotchit finally ratcheted up *his* dedicated job performance.

"Fred, I fully believe you're an impractical, dunce-headed, silly fool!" Scrooge cynically boomed. "Let me hear another asinine peep out of you, and you'll quickly lose your lucrative employment situation with this very successful firm. You're quite a powerful speaker, Fred, when you haughtily fart out of your mouth. I wonder why you don't piss your future away by going into *Parliament* and get your rocks off while eagerly debating William Gladstone, along with his one happy testicle!"

"Please, don't be so nasty and vindictive, Uncle! Come and dine with us tomorrow!" Fred amiably and diplomatically suggested.

"Good afternoon, my misguided Nephew!" Scrooge imperatively answered.

"Uncle, I want you to know I desire nothing from you this Christmas, if you feel compelled to celebrate the holiday without my company," Fred compromised. "Why can't we just be good friends?"

"Good afternoon, my favorite and only Nephew!" Scrooge bitterly repeated. "If you persist in reiterating your frivolous bullshit, then not only is your precious job in immediate jeopardy, but also your grand inheritance as well! Is that scenario perfectly fuckin' clear!"

"I'm sorry with all of my heart and soul to find you so adamant and stubborn about such a joyful phenomenon as Christmas," Fred deliberately antagonized. "I intend to pay homage to Christmas, despite your abundant pessimism and cynicism. And I want you to know that I'll keep my seasonal humor to the very end. So, I must declare, a very Merry Christmas to you, Uncle Scrooge!"

"Get the fuck outa' here, and have a 'good afternoon'!" Scrooge vehemently bellowed.

"And may I genuinely add, a Happy New Year!" Fred optimistically enunciated as the all-too-polite nephew quickly turned and then grabbed the rusty old doorknob.

"Good afternoon!" Scrooge hollered while almost initiating a massive coronary.

Fred left the premises with not a vengeful thought residing inside his benign heart. The idealistic fellow had bravely risked losing his beneficiary status by verbally wrangling with his eccentric, egocentric Uncle Scrooge. Just after the firm's principal procurement officer had departed the dimly-lit office, two portly gentlemen entered the portal, and stood with their hats held against their chests to honor Ebenezer, and to gain his harsh attention. The jovial visitors had arrived with books and documents in their hands. and then one of the soliciting gentlemen rather courteously-but-solemnly addressed the volatile proprietor.

"*Scrooge and Marley's Import and Export*, I believe," the first chubby gentleman stated while checking his extensive list of business names. "Now sir, have I the distinct pleasure of speaking to Mr. Scrooge, or addressing Mr. Marley?"

"Mr. Marley has been dead the past seven years, happening this very night," Scrooge remembered and bitterly replied. "The blundering pecker-head is dead, buried and forgotten."

The second gentleman, realized that his target was going to be a hard sell, so the charity-seeker twice cleared his throat. "At this jubilant time of the year, Mr. Scrooge," the nervous fellow hoarsely articulated, "my associate and I have deemed it desirable that prosperous businessmen such as yourself should make generous donations for the destitute and for the prostitutes, who suffer greatly at this time because the general public spends most of its money on presents, and not on charity or special services." The neurotic solicitor then paused and anxiously applied his pen to his paper to carefully jot-down Scrooge's anticipated humanitarian pledge. "Many thousands are in need of food, shelter, clothing, and drug money," the anxious speaker cited. "And hundreds of thousands are in common need of standard, basic comforts. Many impoverished residents need new houses, and also new horse and buggies."

"Are there no prisons to accommodate these teeming, wasteful parasites who habitually ruin and neglect everything?" Scrooge countered. "What ever happened to traditional begging? Now, the poor-but-cunning shit-heads have commissioned naïve businessmen like you two dimwits to be their surrogate solicitors! I'm fully convinced that the whole world's becoming more-and-more fucked-up every single day!"

"But Mr. Scrooge," the first flustered man interrupted. "Indeed, there are an abundance of overcrowded prisons. But those scandalous institutions cannot possibly furnish adequate Christian cheer when all of the inmates are being sodomized and flogged by their fellow gay inmates, and when they're also constantly being porked up the buttocks by bisexual prison guards and by homosexual wardens. Could you imagine what it's like being a straight inmate and having to daily endure such contemptible, scurrilous abuse?"

"Mr. Scrooge," the now-paranoid, hoarse volunteer butted-in. "A few of us Londoners are attempting to raise a fund to purchase meat, drink, marijuana and cocaine for the impoverished masses. There are mendicants on every street corner just hoping and trying to be arrested so that the exploited masses can be further sodomized in our overcrowded jails. Now then, sir, how much shall I put you down for?"

"Look here, you gullible dumb fucks! We all get wickedly screwed by society and by the bloated government bureaucracy every passing day," Scrooge deftly volleyed. "And if these indigent jerk-offs you're representing get fucked up the ass in filthy prisons, then I don't give a damned, double-somersaulting shit about it. It's a dog-eat-dog world outside the grimy prison, and it's a dog-suck-dog world inside our stupid-assed jails. Those honest facts are permanent and unalterable!"

"I had politely asked how much of a contribution do you intend to make, Mr. Scrooge?" the hoarse, raspy-voiced gentleman asked just before a small frog hopped out of his throat.

"Nothing!" Ebenezer curtly answered.

"Oh, I get it!" the first solicitor exclaimed with a prodigious forced smile. "You're wishing that your generous donation remains anonymous!"

"Look, Mr. Do-Gooder, or whatever your goddamned name is. I wish to be left alone, and not be annoyed or bothered by your picayune bullshit. I don't make merry at Christmas, even if I'm probably the most qualified person in this part of London that could afford indulging in the despicable habit. I do contribute to the prisons and to the workhouses by virtue of my taxes that support such fucked-up institutions," the counting house proprietor curtly added. "And those lazy imbeciles or criminal thugs that are bad off must go to the state's institutions, or work their way up in society as I've so proudly done. Are there any further ludicrous inquiries?"

"But Mr. Scrooge," the appalled hoarse solicitor stammered. "Many gay indigents can't go there, and many straight crooks would rather die!"

"Well, if the dumb-ass, lazy shit-heads would rather die than daily be corn-holed or sodomized in city prisons or workhouses," Scrooge meanly attested, "then the ignoramus dregs had better accomplish it promptly, and thus, diminish the surplus population so that my freakin' taxes will be reduced."

The two, stocky, disgusted gentlemen (who each could easily beat the feces and the urine out of feeble Ebenezer Scrooge) swiftly left the place of business in dual huffs.

The Christmas Eve hour for closing-down the counting house finally arrived. In a pissed-off mood, Ebenezer Scrooge very slowly dismounted his squeaky high stool, which was symbolic communication to Bob Crotchit that the lowly clerk had permission to extinguish his two votive candles and put-out his singular burning miniature coal, which had already-disintegrated into a tiny cinder.

"Well, Crotchit, I suppose you'll want to have tomorrow off all damned day," Ebenezer sneered and snarled. "I'm getting screwed up the ass without even being inside a goddamned prison cell or workhouse!"

"If it will not heavily inconvenience you, sir!" Bob humbly answered.

"It's not convenient, but it *is* indeed rather repugnant to me, and it's certainly not damned fair in the least," Scrooge lividly muttered. "I feel inclined to penalize your ass half a crown for the imposition you're causing me, and you ought to feel guilty about exploiting my vast generosity."

"Yes sir!" subordinate Robert Crotchit obediently acknowledged with his head dejectedly crestfallen, with Bob's fearful eyes lowered and with his pointed chin touching his chest.

"And yet, Crotchit," Scrooge strenuously protested. "You don't in any way think me taken advantage of when I must pay you a day's salary for no work performed. That damned Jacob Marley had to be experiencing temporary insanity when the ass-wiping fool established such a ridiculous policy!"

"It only occurs once a year," the courteous-but-wimpish employee cautiously replied. "Please consider that I wish to spend the joyous and festive holiday with my family."

"A sad excuse for disgracefully picking an honest man's wallet every twenty-fifth of December," Scrooge stubbornly replied as the nasty apostate deliberately refused to say the noun *Christmas*. "Keep your damned dick all to yourself like I do, and then you wouldn't have such an enormous family dependent on your lowly status of employment."

"I intend to do as you suggest in the future, sir," Crotchit reluctantly fibbed. "Yes, I fully intend to sir!"

"Very well, then!" the miserly entrepreneur exclaimed. "But be in this damned office an hour earlier on the 26th!"

The ecstatic clerk promised that he would, and Scrooge re-entered his office wearing something between a frown and a grimace upon his wrinkled countenance. The office was abruptly closed in a London minute, and old Ebenezer watched out the window as his euphoric clerk (wearing a tattered white comforter, with no accompanying greatcoat) slid like a carefree adolescent across a patch of slick ice outside the business establishment's grimy front window. Crotchit then paused at the end of the lane to wish a gathering of boys a genuine "Merry Christmas!" Scrooge shook his head in remote objection to his employee's 'preposterous childish antics'.

Ebenezer Scrooge was in a despondent, uneasy mood as the old geezer ate his melancholy dinner at *his* lonely table inside his usual melancholy tavern. The patron dined alone as was his custom, preferring to judge humanity from afar without ever sharing pleasant thoughts or even 'false cordial greetings'. The isolated diner read the evening newspaper at his favorite corner table, shutting his eyes off from the merriment of the other more-spirited Christmas rcvelers. Then, the old tightwad reluctantly paid his bill, and soon slowly ambled to his apartment suite to thoroughly review his accounting records.

The grumpy old fellow's musty chambers once belonged to his deceased former partner, and the residence constituted three dull rooms in a ramshackle, tenement building. The upstairs' quarters were dreary, dark and cold, especially during the winter. The old coot mechanically climbed-up the all-too-familiar thirteen creaky steps. When fatigued Ebenezer reached his apartment's wooden door, the occupant paused for a moment to scrutinize the metal doorknocker.

It was, at that moment, quite an ordinary-looking doorknocker that was a degree larger than most. Ebenezer was not an imaginative man, and was not prone to have his mind fancifully trespass outside of his narrow thinking perimeter of basically doing business and making profits. But as the old, pessimistic, pitiless tycoon inserted his key into the lock, the dweller perceived a transparent image of Marley's face staring directly at him.

'What the fuck's goin' on here!' Scrooge mentally reacted. 'It's Marley's ugly, pallid sourpuss that looks like an albino lobster present in a white collar. And his glasses are upon his forehead, just as they had always appeared up to seven boring years ago!'

Scrooge vigorously rubbed his bleary eyes, and again peered at the eerie manifestation, but soon, the ghastly, ghostly, pallid face had disappeared, and only the large brass doorknocker could be vaguely perceived. "Pooh, Poop!" Scrooge uttered, shaking his ancient head. "Don't tell me I need new spectacles at my age! I refuse to make the unnecessary investment in such a luxury!"

After Scrooge entered his shadowy, dank foyer, his ears heard a clanging sound ringing throughout the dismal residence, seemingly originating from the casks in the first-floor wine merchant's cellar. But the continuous dissonance greatly disturbed the nasty old cuss. The very audible chain-like rattling echoed and teemed throughout every room, and the sound quickly rose from a dull ringing to a loud clanging. 'My fuckin' ears must be failing too, besides my damned weakened eyes!' the suddenly petrified old fool thought.

The disturbed resident closed the door and double-bolted the lock. Next, Ebenezer trimmed his candle as the recluse cautiously entered the interior of his decrepit quarters. Scrooge loved darkness because he didn't have to pay a penny for it. The miserable occupant carefully walked through his rooms to ascertain that everything was in its proper place, and that nothing had been rearranged or stolen. 'That hideous Jacob Marley ashen face was a goddamned illusion,' Scrooge plausibly explained to himself. 'I need to rest so that after tomorrow passes, the fucked-up world will be back to its old, predictable, normal, fucked-up self!'

Everything was in its exact location as Scrooge closely examined the sitting room; the adjacent lumber-room, and the all-too-familiar bedroom. Ebenezer next cautiously checked under the table and under the sofa, using the light from a small fire in the stove, along with a small handheld votive, to allow the unsettled occupant to inspect and evaluate his coveted possessions.

The spoon and the basin were in their correct positions, and the saucepan of cold soup was still situated upon the hob. No detestable robber was lying under the bed, and no despicable prowler was hiding inside the kitchen. No brutal burglar had been disguised in Ebenezer's dressing gown, which was still hanging in the small wardrobe section of the side closet. 'Every damned thing is in exact order and has not been tampered with!' wary Scrooge begrudgingly concluded.

Quite satisfied with his comprehensive inspection, Scrooge double-locked himself into his bedroom, naturally, to keep-out all possible intruders and trespassers. The fearful fellow removed his cravat, and next tossed his necktie upon the ancient, cedar wood bureau. Then, the distrustful resident removed his clothing and donned his sleeping gown and nightcap. 'Nightcap!' the aged codger thought. 'Yes, perhaps I should calm my nerves and sample a few ounces of blackberry brandy. Not necessarily for me to celebrate the silly Christmas season, but to warm my chest up a bit!' the avaricious nutcase rationalized. The old coot then poured his standard skimpy ounce of sweet liquor into a glass, sat-down in his favorite chair, and leaned back to wallow in his loneliness.

Ebenezer Scrooge's momentary relaxation was instantly interrupted when his ears discerned a bell wildly ringing from the adjoining room. The scared apartment dweller suddenly experienced astonishment and dread, so the old skinflint frantically quaffed-down the last ounce of brandy. His new-found extreme apprehension rapidly converted to fear, and then to awe, as every bell in the dingy tenement house soon rang with great intensity.

Then, a distinct clanking noise was heard, and the sound was akin to a prisoner dragging a heavy ball and chain (around his foot) across the floor. The disturbing distraction seemed to be originating from the wine merchant's warehouse situated below Scrooge's less-than-mundane apartment. The very unnerving interruption was next coming from the outside steps, and its presence was gradually moving towards the entrance to Scrooge's lackluster residence. The weird noise, accompanied by a specter's pale outline, instantaneously passed though the sidewall, and horribly confronted the shocked tycoon right in the center of *his* unkempt bedroom.

"I know you!" Scrooge attested in utter amazement. "You're Jacob Marley's ghost!"

Indeed, it was Marley's gruesome face; Marley's trademark pigtail dangling-down, and Marley's waistcoat, boots and tights. But the fellow's body was whitish and translucent, and the ashen-looking image had just approached Scrooge by filtering through a dense opaque wall. The two buttons upon Marley's waistcoat seemed to be on the backside of *his* flat form, rather than on the front where the objects rightfully belonged.

'Marley has no damned bowels, just as others had often suspected when the repugnant bastard was alive!' Scrooge's cynical mind conjectured, while his fearful eyes studied the ghost's invisible abdomen. 'But now it looks like he's not at all full of shit as everyone had thought,' Ebenezer imagined. 'I don't at all believe *this* abnormal trick, or prank that I'm witnessing. It's got to be a lot of hostile humbug or bull-crap!'

Scrooge regained some of his composure and meticulously examined the enigmatic phantom through and through. His senses felt its chilling influence, despite the fact that *that feeling* was ordinarily alien to *his* icy nature. The apparition's stark, morbid, death-cold-eyes seemed to be peering right through Ebenezer, in the same manner as Scrooge's acute vision was seeing directly through the very transparent ghost. The appalled local merchant stood with his jaws agape, analyzing in detail the morose two-dimensional specter.

"What the hell do you want?" Scrooge nervously asked his uninvited guest. "Why do you haunt my skinny ass?"

"I want quite much!" Marley's unique voice demanded. "And watch how *you* loosely use that word 'hell'. It's not a desirable place to spend eternity, I quite assure you!"

"Well then," the very astounded Scrooge carefully continued. "May I ask who *you* really are?"

"Ask me who I once *was* would certainly constitute a much better and more accurate question of plausible interrogation!" the blunt specter mysteriously clarified.

"Well then, who *were* you?" the withered geezer neurotically asked the mystic intruder.

"In life, I was your partner, Jacob Marley. Listening to that gay reggae music was only my most minor fault," the itinerant spirit solemnly jested. "Now, Ebenezer, I'm even more cheerless and depressed than when I had *lived,* if I should recklessly misuse *that* word."

"Can you, can you sit down?" Scrooge stuttered with his confidence clearly shaken.

"I can, but actually don't need to," the ghost convincingly replied. "Honestly, I have no more sensation in my ass, and know not the joys of comfort or pleasure."

Scrooge was asking a litany of irrelevant questions in order to stall for time to retrieve his superior attitude that had temporarily abandoned him during his extreme anxiety. Although still extraordinarily afraid, the somewhat-curious tenant felt compelled to seek some logical explanations concerning the nature of the arcane afterworld. The stern ghost parked his transparent buttocks upon the opposite side of the stone fireplace.

"You don't believe in me, or understand my present existence," Marley's spirit asked. "You've always been a deceitful doubter!"

"I don't!" Scrooge defiantly and obstinately answered. "You might be a lousy damned undigested bit of tavern beef that's affecting my friggin' senses, or perhaps a rancid crumb of cheese, or perhaps some mustard vilely irritating my weak stomach, or maybe an undercooked fragment of a foul, baked potato," the aged codger speculated and related. "I believe that this ordeal is some kind of tremendous hoax, and that there's more of gravy than of morbid grave about you, Mr. Jacob Marley, alien Ghost Impostor!"

Scrooge was not a habitual joke teller, so his clumsy commentary was really very much out of character for his selfish, natural demeanor. The stunned-and-beleaguered skeptic was simply attempting to gain the upper-hand in his conversation with his spooky guest by attempting to re-establish the miser's standard pessimistic, reprehensible, narcissistic, totally condescending, very egotistical, contemptible, superior self. Ebenezer's instinct was to diminish the horror that was effectively dominating his thoughts and actions.

The phantom removed the lengthy bandage from its hideous-looking head, and its lower jaw dropped-down to its chest to signify its disgust for Scrooge's excessive arrogance. The ominous shade then peered at its host with penetrating eyes that scared the unholy hell out of Ebenezer Scrooge.

"Mercy, wretched occult specter!" Scrooge exhorted in a trembling voice. "Why must you fuckin' torture my soul, and why must you fuckin' come to me in the middle of the damned night?"

"If I were you, Ebenezer Scrooge," the ghost grimly counseled, "I would refrain from using pedestrian profanity to awkwardly disguise your insecurity. I've recently checked your human ledger, and your remaining days are especially numbered. And truly, I've come to enlighten you that you still have some sand left in your hourglass to wholly reform your life, and to avoid *my* horrendous fate. As it is right now, Ebenezer," the spirit curtly cautioned and counseled, "you're dooming yourself to an eternal fate that is far worse than mine."

"But why must you walk the earth in those monstrous chains?" the counting house owner nervously asked. "Why Jacob?"

"Each link in these chains represents a bad habit that I had foolishly exercised when I unfortunately-but-voluntarily breathed and lived, just like yourself, as an inconsiderate and despicable human being," the apparition guiltily informed. "This link represents my greed; and this one my avarice; and this one my stinginess; and this one is my merciless exploitation of others; and this one is my pride; and this one is my scorn for humanity, and this one, must I go on?" Marley's saddened and penitent ghost asked.

"But why must you awkwardly travel the world with such stifling encumbrance?" Scrooge awkwardly wanted to know.

"Because I have no *damned* choice in the matter," the ghost regretfully related. "I reluctantly surrendered my free will the moment I took my last breath. And I'm now trapped in a wicked void, somewhere between limbo and purgatory, until I adequately fulfill all the assignments that have been given to me. I haven't even met any of the higher-ups in the afterlife yet? I only take strict instructions from minor angels!"

"Will you stay and tell me everything you know about death?" Scrooge inquired. "I'm approaching that ugly threshold, as you well know!"

"I'm strictly permitted to tell you little more than I've already revealed," the apparition honestly disclosed. "I cannot rest until my eighty-year post burial mission is fulfilled, for my punishment amounts to the number of years I had wasted my former life upon *your* earth. I trudge and wander around, seeking-out the borderline souls that still might be salvaged. When I had sinfully lived," the mournful ghost stated with great emphasis and sorrow about his colossal burden, "I scarcely ever traveled anywhere outside of London. I, like you, Ebenezer Scrooge, never visited others in need, or made their responsibilities seem lighter to endure. I, just like you are now, had been a totally self-centered, egotistical asshole!"

"What do you miss the most?" Scrooge hesitantly asked. "There must be something! Eating? Counting money?"

"I greatly miss human companionship and compassion," the macabre specter instantly admitted. "I do, to a minor degree, miss eating, breathing, and basic physical pleasures. As a roaming ghost, I possess only a pale two-dimensional, vaporous form. I miss the body's urge to have pleasure, even though I shunned and ridiculed the practice when I had lived."

"Seven years nomadically trekking the earth is a very long time," Scrooge marveled and expressed as the observer bravely stuck his hand throw Marley's ghost's two-dimensional form to verify that the image indeed was of a supernatural nature. "Indeed, friend Jacob, you must've traversed a great expanse of land in *that* recent seven-year time frame."

"Oh, Ebenezer Scrooge," the pale figure objectively and impersonally replied. "What a poor blind man you are, even with your current perfect vision! Your heart is cold and apathetic when it comes down to fathoming the futile pleas of the less fortunate. You abhor Christian spirit, and your black heart despises good will towards mankind!" the spirit explained. "You condemn all that is good and constructive for the soul's nourishment! And yes, I was once a facsimile of you, Ebenezer Scrooge. I was once a dysfunctional ditto of your chronic abhorrent misbehavior!"

"But Jacob, you were always a good man of business, honest as the day is long," Scrooge ineffectively debated. "You never fuckin' cheated a man out of a penny, once a deal to your satisfaction had been negotiated!"

"I've already told you to watch your indiscriminate choice of words," the other-world visitor again admonished. "You neglect to comprehend that mankind was my business; that charity was my business; that mercy was my business; that forgiveness was my business, and that benevolence was my business. Our accounting firm was only *our livelihood,* whose profits you and I never shared with anyone, including our immediate families! Both you and I had always been dreadful, conniving, abrasive, reprehensible, intolerable shit-heads, who incessantly used to read graphic porno' magazines!"

At that juncture, Ebenezer Scrooge's mind was very much puzzled, and his normally confident demeanor was suddenly immersed in a vast quandary. The devious miser began trembling as if his body had been afflicted by St. Vitus disease and major Parkinson's.

"Hear my words, Ebenezer," Marley's ghost austerely implored. "Hear and honor my final words to you, and heed their significance!"

"I shall, dear Jacob, I shall!" the frightened listener impetuously concurred. "But please don't be too flowery or mushy in your vivid descriptions, my dear Jacob. I had always distrusted your effeminate nature, and felt that you had suppressed, latent, homosexual tendencies, whenever I noticed either Fred or Bob Crotchit feeling gay and blithe.”

“I’ve deliberately sought you out tonight, Ebenezer, to advise that you still may satisfactorily redeem your reprehensible, mortal existence,” Marley’s Ghost sternly declared. “You still have an opportunity to save your eternal soul through the sincere exercise of a benevolent free will, which may still cancel-out your past abominations.”

“Jacob Marley, you were always a *damned* good friend, ally and business associate,” Scrooge readily admitted. “Thank you, Jacob; thank you very much!”

“Tonight, sir, I’m but a hopeful courier. I must convey that you’re to be soon visited and haunted by three special separate-but-unique spirits!” Marley’s Ghost sanctimoniously divulged. “Those three just mentioned and predicted specters will profoundly influence and promote your spiritual development!”

"Is that the stupid-assed only chance of redemption your wisdom offers me?" Scrooge assertively challenged. "I think I'd rather go to bed and dream about getting laid and losing my damned virginity, or about increasing my wealth, than be pestered and cajoled by three offensive ghosts."

"What did I tell you about loosely using obscenities and vulgar language!" the ghost seriously again chastised. "You cannot evade a parallel fate as my own unless you fully cooperate with the three alluded-to spirits, and then faithfully and obediently honor their vital recommendations. If you fail to comply, then eternal damnation will most certainly be your ultimate punishment."

"At which hours will these three visiting apparitions arrive to haunt my vulnerable soul?" Scrooge wondered and asked.

"You can expect the first tomorrow morning when the church bells toll one. Anticipate the second shade when the bells peal three. Expect the third when the toll rings five. And for your own blessed sake, and I do mean *blessed* sake," Marley's Ghost quite discreetly and specifically emphasized, "loyally remember to obediently follow all divine advice that is demanded of you."

Marley's Ghost then stood-up from the hearth's stone ledge, and with its frightful eyes focused directly upon Scrooge, the apparition eerily floated backwards through the wall, attached rattling ball, chains, and all. The frail, deserted man rubbed his eyes to ascertain that he had not hallucinated what his believing pupils had just witnessed.

Being a fairly agnostic creature of constant doubt, unscrupulous Scrooge examined the door to confirm that the object had indeed been double-locked prior to the wayward ghost's astounding incursion into his apartment. 'The bolts are undisturbed, but conversely, my mind *is* deeply disturbed!' Scrooge solemnly acknowledged while experiencing a minor panic attack. The dubious miser endeavored to utter 'Humbug!' but his parched tongue could not even complete the first syllable.

And perhaps it was because of his recent great supernatural ordeal, or because of the late hour of the night, Ebenezer Scrooge slowly plopped into his flimsy bed, which the elderly fool immediately recognized as being a temporary safe haven.

'I just had a perverted contact with the obscure, invisible world that I dreadfully fear!' the intimidated capitalist pondered. 'If I fall asleep, I might not wake up! I'll just restlessly sit in my bed, and wait for the first promised ghost's haunting,' the disheveled egotist reckoned. 'It's much better *to live* in this damned world and be mischievously haunted, than to live a dead existence in the next *damned* world, and have to perpetually roam the earth, cruelly assigned to mercilessly haunt a conniving, former friend.'

Jay Dubya

Stave Two
"The First of the Three Spirits"

When Scrooge abruptly awoke in a terribly confused state of mind, the room was so dark, that, looking from his archaic bed, Old Geezer Ebenezer could scarcely distinguish the transparent window from the opaque walls of his bleak chamber, until suddenly, the distant church tower clock tolled a deep, bass, hollow, melancholy ONE.

Bright light instantly flashed-up inside the room, and the dusty curtains of Ebenezer's bed were instantly drawn aside by a strange figure, seemingly like a child: yet not so like a child as like an old, withered man, whom viewed through some glowing supernatural medium, gave the cryptic apparition the appearance of having receded from the astounded spectator's view. And after being gradually diminished to a mere child's proportions, the specter's hair, which hung about its neck and down its back, was pure white as if with age. And yet, the new arrival's face had not a wrinkle upon it, and the tenderest bloom was apparent upon the skin.

The mysterious phantom held a branch of fresh green holly in its left hand and, in singular contradiction of *that* wintry emblem, had its dress (Scrooge imagined the weird visitor as being some sort a transvestite phenomenon) trimmed with summer flowers. But truly, the strangest aspect about the illuminated, eerie guest was, that from the crown of its head, there sprung a bright clear jet of light, by which all this incredible spectacle was entirely visible.

"Are you, Spirit, the one whose coming had been recently foretold to me by deceased Jacob Marley's Ghost?"

"I am! And I've been designated and assigned to visit you; you pathetic, shrinking, primitive fossil!"

"Who and what the hell are you?"

"Watch your vulgar language, Ebenezer Scrooge. You had meant to say, 'Who and what the *Heaven* are you'? Well now, I am the

Ghost of Christmas Past, if you are wondering about my present wandering."

"Long past?"

"No, Dumb-ass. Your past. The scenes that you'll soon see with me are pertinent shadows of the things that have already transpired; however, the events, or their personages, will have no consciousness of *our* presence."

Scrooge then made bold to inquire what business brought the Ghost of Christmas Past to his drab and dingy apartment.

"Your welfare, Mr. Scrooge. Even though you're a rich and greedy bastard, your welfare is my current mission. Get your ass up off your lackluster bed. Rise, I demand, and walk along with me!"

Although Old Geezer Ebenezer possessed mostly *pedestrian* ideas and notions, it would have been in vain for Scrooge to plead that the weather and the hour were not especially adapted to pedestrian purposes. His familiar bed was fairly warm, and the window's external thermometer indicated a temperature that was reading way below freezing.

The parsimonious curmudgeon was lightly clad in his shabby fur slippers, his shoddy and thin porno' dressing-gown, along with his rather cumbersome nightcap. And the aged codger had been suffering from a wicked head cold at that time. The ghost's grasp, though gentle as a woman's soft hand, was not to be resisted. Scrooge reluctantly rose, but finding that the Spirit made a motion towards the frosted window, instinctively clasped the specter's robe in apparent supplication.

"I am a mortal, and liable to fall and be mortally wounded."

"Bear but a touch of my comforting hand," the occult visitor instructed, laying *his* right palm upon his heart. "And you shall be upheld in more than this gesture! We'll glide and speed across the passage of time, for although it is midnight, I assure you, this will not be any fly-by-night operation!"

As those almost-incredulous words were spoken, the pair majestically passed through the apartment's solid wall, and soon stood in a busy thoroughfare of the hectic city. It was made plain by simple observation, enough by a cursory scrutiny of the dressing of the various retail shops, that here, too, it was Christmas time, but certainly a holiday being very emblematic of an earlier time.

"Your welfare is my mission," the Ghost firmly communicated. "And don't answer me back, foolishly insisting you don't desire or accept any monetary *welfare* from anyone!"

Scrooge expressed himself much obliged, but could not help thinking that a night of unbroken rest would certainly have been more conducive to having awkward conversation with a totally remarkable spiritual entity. To Scrooge's inferior comprehension, the spooky visitor must have possessed mental telepathy skills and amazingly heard him thinking, for the shade immediately stated: "Your rather personal reclamation, Ebenezer Scrooge. Take heed of my direct commands, you, stubborn, mediocre, ignorant knucklehead."

The rather mysterious Ghost of Christmas Past put-out its strong right hand as it spoke with powerful authority, and next persuasively clasped his aged companion gently by the arm. "Rise your spine erect, obstinate old man. And don't dare resist walking with me."

In a miraculous flash, the pair stood upon an open country road, with fallow farm fields prevalent on either side. Astonishingly, the hustle and bustle of the city avenue had entirely vanished. Not a vestige of detectable London Town was to be seen. The former darkness and mist had vanished with it, for now it was a clear, cold, winter day, with sheets of ice and a blanket snow evident upon the frozen ground.

"Good Heaven!" flustered Scrooge yelped, clasping his hands together, as the elderly coot staggered and looked about him. "I was bred in the exact vicinity of this very place. I was a boy here."

The Spirit mildly gazed upon his mortal companion. The ethereal guide's gentle touch, although it had been light and instantaneous, appeared still present to the old man's sense of feeling. Ebenezer's nostrils were conscious of a thousand odors variously floating-about in the air, with each one connected with a thousand thoughts, hopes, and joys, and each nostril impression also, carrying memorable cares, all long, long, forgotten.

"Your parched lips are trembling," the benign Ghost verbally observed and indicated. "And what is that distinct moisture trickling and cascading down upon your cheek?"

Scrooge uncomfortably muttered, with an unusual stutter apparent in his voice, that it was a liquid pimple; and the wily prevaricator begged the courteous Ghost to carefully lead him wherever he would.

"You recollect the exact way?" the Ghost of Christmas Past inquired.

"Remember it!" Scrooge acknowledged with obvious fervor. "To this very day, I could easily trek the whole path blindfolded."

"Strange to have forgotten it for so many years," observed and articulated the Ghost. "Let us go on, for my time is scant."

The duo paced along the frozen dirt road, with Scrooge recognizing and remembering every gate, post, and tree; until a little market-town appeared in the perceptible distance, featuring its bridge, its church, and winding river exactly as Ebenezer's memory accurately recollected. Some shaggy ponies were now seen trotting towards *their* presence, with excited boys saddled upon their backs, who called to other lads situated in country gigs, wagons, and carts, all driven by merry farmers.

"These depictions are but shadows of the things that have been," the Ghost blandly revealed. "They have no consciousness of us being here."

The jovial natives rambled-by, and as the jolly villagers moved about their activities, Scrooge recalled and named each one. Why was the London recluse rejoiced beyond all bounds, simply to see them? Why did his cold eyes glisten, and his heart leap-up as his former juvenile acquaintances merrily sped past? Why was Ebenezer filled with gladness when his ears heard them genuinely declaring to each other "A very Merry Christmas", as the happy youngsters parted at cross-roads and by-ways in the middle of the usually somnolent village, heading towards their separate homes? What was in *that* delightful past portrayal of "Merry Christmas" that had been connected to Scrooge in his later lifetime? Indeed, it contradicted his patented enunciation, "Out upon Merry Christmas"! What good had its sacred homage ever done, either to or for him?

"The school is not quite deserted," the omniscient Ghost casually related. "A solitary child, momentarily neglected by his boisterous friends, is left alone, waiting there, still."

Scrooge admitted that he knew and remembered the experience. And his eyes again teared-up, and the old recaller sobbed.

The unique pair of time-traveling witnesses magically left the high-road, floated above a well-remembered lane, and soon approached a mansion of faded red brick, featuring a little rusty weathercock, surmounted above a cupola upon the roof, and a rusty school-bell hanging inside it. The edifice was a fairly large schoolhouse, but one of broken fortunes; for the spacious offices were presently little used;

their walls were damp and mossy; their windows cracked, and the aged building's gates somewhat decayed.

Fowls clucked and strutted inside the nearby stables, and the coach-houses and sheds were over-run with wild grass and tall weeds. Nor was it more retentive of its ancient state, within; for entering the dreary main hall, and glancing through the open doors of several classrooms, the time and space travelers found the structure's features poorly furnished, especially cold, and quite vast. There persisted an earthy savor within the air; a chilly bareness seemingly inhabited the memorable place, which associated itself in Scrooge's vivid recollection as somehow existing with too much studying by dim candle-light, and a memory of having not too much food to eat.

The Ghost and Scrooge ventured across the hall, and stepped to a door at the back of the old schoolhouse. The solid object mystically opened before them, and disclosed a long, bare, melancholy chamber, made barer still by lines of rather plain tables and dusty desks. At one of those seats, a lonely boy impatiently sat quietly reading near a weak fire, and Scrooge peered-down and sat upon a chair, and wept while seeing his poor forgotten self as his impatient existence used to appear in a mirror in his early youth.

Not even a latent echo could be discerned inside the ramshackle schoolhouse; not a squeak nor a minor scuffle had been detected from the mice behind the warped paneling; not a drip from the half-thawed water-pump in the dull yard behind; not a sigh among the leafless boughs of one outside rotting poplar; and not the idle swinging of an empty store-house door was discernible; no, but the silent mirage seemed all too surreal.

The accommodating mystic Spirit touched Ebenezer upon the arm, and pointed to *his* younger self, the lonely lad sadly intent upon his leisurely reading. Suddenly, an adolescent, in foreign garments: wonderfully real and distinct to look at, stood outside the window, with an axe stuck in his belt, and leading a donkey laden with wood.

"Why, it's Ali Baba!" Scrooge exclaimed in momentary ecstasy. "It's dear, old, honest Ali Baba without his imaginary seven thieves. Yes, yes, I vividly recall. Upon One Christmas time, when yonder solitary child was left here all alone, he did come, for the first time, just like that. Poor boy. And Valentine," Scrooge verbalized, "and his wild brother, Orson; there the two friends go strolling down the icy lane. Dear Ghost? Am I now having a sort of 'Road to Damascus' experience?"

To hear Scrooge expending all the earnestness of his adult nature on such minute subjects, described in a most extraordinary voice, a tone vacillating between laughing and crying; and to see his heightened and excited face, would have certainly been a surprise to his pompous business associates gathered in the city, indeed.

"There's the familiar classroom Parrot," Scrooge ecstatically cried. "Green body and yellow tail, with a flap like a lettuce leaf growing out of the top of his head; yes, there he is! 'Poor Robin Crusoe', we called him, when his imaginary master came home again after exploring around the island. Poor Robin Crusoe, where have you been, Robin Crusoe? You had invented the five-day work week because you had all of your labor done by Friday! Ha, ha, ha!"

The aged man thought he was dreaming, but in truth, Scrooge wasn't. It was undoubtedly the Parrot, Robin Crusoe that young Ebenezer's bleary eyes were perceiving and reading about. "Yes, there goes Friday, now running for his life to the little island creek! Hallo! Hoop! Hallo!"

Then, with a rapidity of transition that was very foreign to his usual acerbic character, Scrooge recalled and emotionally reflected, in pity, for his former self, "Poor neglected boy!" and his lips whimpered again.

"I wish," Scrooge muttered, putting his hand inside his tattered pants pocket, and looking about his childhood environment, after drying his eyes with his cuff: "But I regret that it's all too late now to alter."

"What is the matter?" the Spirit politely asked. "You definitely seem emotionally uncomfortable!"

"Nothing special nor major," Scrooge answered and hesitated. "Nothing. There was a boy singing a Christmas Carol at my door last night. I should like to have given him something to reward his effort: that's all."

The pleasant Ghost smiled thoughtfully, and waved its mighty and potent hand, saying as it did so, "Let us see another Christmas!"

Scrooge's former self grew larger at the pronouncement of those imperative words, and the room became a little darker and dirtier. The panels cryptically shrunk; the windows cracked; fragments of plaster fell-out of the ceiling, and the naked laths were shown instead. But how all that unfathomable magic was being brought about, Scrooge knew no explanation. The befuddled fellow only knew that it all was quite correct in presentation; that everything had happened so precisely; that there he was, seated alone, in isolation again, when all the other classmates had gone home for the festive holiday season.

The observer's former self was not reading now, but pacing-up and down the classroom, despairingly. Scrooge looked indulgently at the benevolent Ghost, and with a mournful shaking of his perplexed head, glanced anxiously towards the door.

The portal squeakily opened, and a little girl, much younger than the abandoned boy, came darting in, and putting her arms about his neck, often vigorously kissing him, and lovingly addressing young Ebenezer as being her "Dear, dear brother".

"I have gladly come to bring you home, dear brother!" the affectionate girl sincerely declared, clapping her tiny hands, and bending-down to indulgently laugh. "To bring you home, home, home!"

"Home, little Fran?" gratefully returned her rather thrilled sibling.

"Yes!" enthusiastically verified the gleeful sister, brimming with absolute joy. "Home, for good. Home, for ever and ever, Ebenezer.

Father is now so much kinder than he used to be, that *our* home's now like wonderful Heaven! Our father spoke so gently to me one dear night when I was going to bed, that I was not afraid to ask him once more if you might come home; and he replied "Yes", and he, just fifteen-minutes ago, sent me in a coach to bring and escort you' back. Father has quite mellowed, and I believe has had a favorable change of heart toward you. And kind brother, you're now transformed in *his* eyes to be a fine young man!" Fran emphasized, opening her eyes wide. "And you're never to come back to this terrible country boarding school again. You'll never again be horribly separated from me. But first, Ebenezer, we're to be happily together all the Christmas long, and we'll have the most blissful time in all the world."

"You're sounding like quite a grown lady, little Fran!" the euphoric lad exclaimed.

Fran again excitedly clapped her hands, laughed, and tried to touch young Ebenezer's head; but being too short in stature, giggled again, and stood on tiptoes to embrace his waist. Then, the overly ecstatic sister began energetically dragging him, in her childish eagerness, towards the wooden schoolroom door, and eagerly, the brother cooperatively accompanied her.

A formidable and austere voice in the hallway loudly bellowed, "Bring-down Master Scrooge's box, there!" And in the corridor appeared the stern and inflexible schoolmaster himself, whose eyes glared upon Master Scrooge with a ferocious condescension, and the extremely grim stare threw Ebenezer-the-intimidated-student into a dreadful state of mind by coldly shaking hands goodbye with the domineering pedagogue.

"Your sister Fran was always a delicate creature, whom a breath might have easily withered," the very knowledgeable Ghost of Christmas Past explained. "But obviously, Fran had always maintained a compassionate, generous heart!"

"So wonderfully precious Fran indeed had been," Scrooge concurred in a saddened voice.

"You're right. I'll not gainsay it, Spirit. God forbid me ever criticizing her integrity!"

"She later died as a grown woman," the Ghost bluntly stated. "And she had, as I think, children."

"One child," Scrooge mournfully returned. "A boy!"

"True," the Ghost confirmed. "Your loyal, jovial nephew!"

Scrooge seemed uneasy within his mind at *that* particular reminder, and answered briefly, "Yes. My faithful nephew, Fred."

Although the ethereal visitors had at *that* exact moment magically left the country schoolhouse far behind them, the time and space trekkers were now again ambling-around in the busy thoroughfares of the city, where shadowy passengers passed and repassed; where noisy carts and coaches battled for the right-of-way, and where all the strife and tumult of a real, competitive metropolis existed and thrived on a daily basis. It was made plain enough, by the seasonal dressing of the shops, that here too, it was

Christmastime, but the time of day was evening, and the streets were lighted-up.

The Ghost suddenly halted their forward progress at a certain warehouse door, and asked Scrooge if he knew its singular identity.

"Know it! I was happily apprenticed here during my youth? Why must you persist in haunting me with this nostalgic, stark vision?"

The oddball duo stepped through the wall as if by osmosis. Ebenezer's dazzled eyes quickly sighted an old gentleman attired in a Welsch wig, who was sitting behind such a high desk that, if the old fart had been two inches taller, the odd fellow could have knocked his hideous head against the beamed ceiling. Scrooge cried-out in great excitement: "Why, it's old Fuzzybush! Bless his charitable heart. It's my mentor Fuzzybush, and the flamboyant bonehead is alive again!"

Old Fuzzybush methodically laid-down his pen, and being exceedingly anxious, looked-up at the grandfather clock, which incidentally had no grandkids. The dependable timepiece pointed to the hour of seven. Fuzzybush rubbed his hands together in pure delight, adjusted his capacious, wasteful waistcoat, laughed all over himself, from his shoes to his flaccid organ of benevolence (wherever the hell that was), and called-out in a veritably comfortable, oily, rich, fat, merry voice: "Yo ho, there! You, Ebenezer! You, Dick, er, I mean you, Richard Wilkins! And also, you, Master Bates. Er, I mean Tom Bates"

A living and moving picture of Scrooge's former self instantly appeared from the surrounding shadows, indeed a handsome young man, who came ambling briskly inside the grand room, accompanied by his two fellow-apprentices.

"That's young Dick Wilkins, to be sure!" Scrooge exclaimed to the rather bored Ghost. "My old fellow-prentice, bless me, yes. There he is. He was very much attached to me, was Dick. Poor Dick! Dear, dear! And Master Bates had a dick, too!"

"Yo ho, my dear boys!" bellowed a half-intoxicated Fuzzybush in a boisterously jolly manner. "No more arduous work to-night. It's

Christmas Eve, Dick and Tom. Christmas Eve, Ebenezer! Let's have the shutters pulled-up, before a man can say Andrew Jackson; er, I mean Jackie Robinson; er, I mean Robinson Crusoe; er, I mean Jack Robinson! Clear away, my lads, and let's have lots of room here to conduct a gay, er, I mean, to have a fantastic heterosexual party! I don't hire any Tom, Dick or Ebenezer, you know, ha ha ha!"

Clear away the dusty desks and chairs! Certainly, there was nothing the employees wouldn't have cleared-away, or couldn't have cleared-away, with old Ludwig Fuzzybush looking on. The furniture was efficiently moved to the corners in less than a Manchester minute. Every bit of clutter was packed-off, as if the various items were being dismissed from public life forevermore. The planked floor was meticulously swept, cleaned, and watered; the lamps were readily trimmed; ample fuel was heaped upon the fire, and the dilapidated warehouse was as snug and warm, and as dry and bright a ball-room as you would desire to see upon a cold winter's night.

In came a fiddler with a wrinkled music-book, and the musician merrily sauntered-up to the lofty desk. And the animated bloke, who played second fiddle to no one, creatively made an orchestra of it, and the comical gent expertly tuned his instrument, the object sounding like fifty stomach-aches. In came Mrs. Fuzzybush, (who no longer possessed a fuzzy bush), with her countenance featuring one vast substantial smile. In came the six Miss Fuzzybushes, with their fuzzy bushes concealed under heavy woolen dresses. In came their six suitors (all studying to be tailors), whose hearts the six female teasers often broke.

Next, in came all the young men and women employed in the secret upstairs bordello business. In came the obnoxious horny housemaid, with her cousin the kinky trans-baker. In came the cook, with her brother's particular drunken friend, the sex-addict local milkman. In came the rest of the neighborhood assholes, entering one after another; some shyly, some boldly, some gracefully, some marching awkwardly, some pushing, some pulling, and some egregiously farting; in the stupid-shits all rambunctiously came, anyhow and everyhow.

And incredibly, away they all went, twenty couples zipping-around at once; hands half-around and back again; soon, the other way; down the middle and up again; around and around in various stages of recreational grouping and silly groping; old top couple always turning-up in the wrong place; new top couple starting-off again, as soon as the dance participants had ineptly and clumsily gotten there; all top couples at last, and not a bottom one to assist in making the nutcase prancers' general disorganization look proper.

When that wild activity was finally brought to a close, old Fuzzybush, clapping his hands to stop the extensive dance, cried-out, "Well done! Just like I prefer my steak prepared! Oh, fiddlesticks! Now kind fiddler, stop fiddling-around, and don't you dare go playing your instrument up on the roof!" And without instruction, the neurotic fiddler aggressively

plunged his hot, sweaty face into a pot
of imported porter, which had especially been
provided for *that* festive ceremony's purpose
by the company's porter.

The perfunctory hopping and skipping was
soon followed by more prolific dancing, and
there were forfeits, four fits, and more dances,
and there was cake, and there was a great piece
of Cold Roast; and there was a great piece of
Cold Boiled, and not mincing words, there
were mince-pies, and plenty of fresh beer,
since immense happiness had been brewing.
But the great effect of the evening came after
the delicious "Roast and Boiled" had been
consumed, when the fiddler struck-up the top
forty classic hit, "Sir Roger de Coverley".

Then, old Ludwig Fuzzybush stood-out to
dance with Mrs. Fuzzybush, whose, as has
been mentioned, pubic area was no longer
fuzzy. Top couple, too; with a good stiff piece
of work cut-out for them; three or four and
twenty pair of partners; people who were not
to be trifled with; people who would dance,
and had no notion of walking, strolling,

cavorting, sauntering, pacing, meandering, or intentionally or accidentally urinating upon the wood-planked floor, since everyone involved in the frivolous ritual was wearing a dense, dependable, baby diaper.

But if the attendees had been twice as many revelers, old Fuzzybush would have been a perfect match for them, and so would matchless Mrs. Fuzzybush. As to her, the corpulent woman was worthy to be her husband's partner in every sense of the term. A positive light appeared to issue from Fuzzybush's enormous calves as the inelegant imbecile swiftly rotated-around the cluttered, converted workroom. His sparkling, hairy legs splendidly shone and glittered in every segment of the dance. You couldn't have predicted, at any given time, what would become of the enthralled couple next, with perhaps Fuzzybush's obese calves winding-up in a country cow pasture. And when old Ludwig and Mrs. Fuzzybush had gone all through their intricate dance maneuvers, advance and retire, turn your partner, bow and courteously curtsy, corkscrew, thread the needle, and back again to their respective place, Fuzzybush "cut", cut so deftly, that the zany fuck appeared to be redundantly winking with his swollen legs.

When the room's clock struck eleven, that dynamic, domestic ball gradually broke-up. Mr. and Mrs. Fuzzybush took their stations, one on either side of the exit door, and, shaking hands with every person individually as he or she cheerfully departed the premises, wished him or her a "Merry Christmas". When everybody had retired except the three apprentices, the jubilant owner of the firm did the same to them; and thus, the cheerful voices gradually died-away, and the three lads were left to their beds, which were situated under a filthy counter inside the back shop.

"A small matter," the Ghost of Christmas Past articulated, "to make these ordinary folks so full of gratitude. Your former boss has spent but a few pounds of your mortal money, three or four perhaps. Is that so much a sum that he deserves *this* obvious and abundant praise and appreciation?"

"It isn't *that* mundane deduction," Scrooge declared, irritated by the specter's relevant narrative. And speaking unconsciously like *his* former, not his latter self, "It isn't that, most-annoying Spirit. Fuzzybush had the power to render us either happy or unhappy; to make our service light or burdensome; either a pleasure or a toil. Say that his enormous power lies in words and looks; in deeds so slight and insignificant that it is impossible to add and count them up: what then? The happiness he gives is quite as great as if his effort cost a fantastic fortune."

Scrooge's perception felt the Spirit's penetrating glance, and stopped.

"What is the matter?"

"Nothing in particular."

"Something significant, I think? You're acting rather fucked-up!"

"You claim to be a heavenly messenger, yet you use vulgar language!" Ebenezer challenged.

"Fuck-off, bro'!" the greatly insulted Spirit replied. "Morality is just designed for humans. I'm an immortal ghost, and I'm not subject to your bull-shit requirements to safely enter into the hereafter."

"So why am I here in Fuzzybush's old factory? What am I *here after?*"

"You're rehearsing for your upcoming audition in front of the Almighty? What kind of idiotic jerk-off are you, Ebenezer Scrooge?"

"No, no, Spirit. I should like to be able to say a word or two to *my* reliable clerk, Bob Crotchit, just now. That's all."

"My time schedule with you grows short," the Spirit pertinently observed and starkly commented. "Please remember, you are not *presently* in your place of business. You are maneuvering in the past at your former boss's trading business. Quick!"

This informative lecture was not addressed to Scrooge, or to any one whom Ebenezer could see, but its declaration produced an immediate effect. For once again, befuddled Scrooge saw himself as a vision. The wealthy spendthrift was quite older now; a bachelor in the prime of life. Ebenezer was not alone, but sat by the side of an attractive young girl wearing a black dress, in whose eyes there were abundant tears.

"It matters little," the pretty maiden softly remarked to Scrooge's former self. "To you, Ebenezer, it matters very little. Another idol has displaced me; and if it can adequately comfort you in times to come, as I would have tried to do, I have no just cause to grieve."

"I don't fully fathom your words, Belle," the worried suitor asked. "Pray tell, what Idol has wickedly displaced you as my wonderful bride to be?"

"A golden one. You fear the world too much, Ebenezer Scrooge. I have seen your nobler aspirations fall-off by the wayside, one by one, until the master-passions, Gain, Greed and Mammon, have fully engrossed you; have I not witnessed such?"

"What then? Even if I have grown so much wiser and materialistic with maturity, what then? I am not changed towards you, Belle. I am still an honest man. Have I ever sought release from our engagement?"

"In words, no. Never! But my experience with you lately has shown that you are both avaricious and covetous in regard to obtaining excessive wealth and property."

"In what, then. Please explain to me the circumstances? Would you rather be poor?"

In a changed nature; in an altered spirit; in another atmosphere of extreme, egotistical life; another selfish Hope that your hungry heart possesses as its great end. If you were free to-day, to-morrow, yesterday, can even I believe that you would choose a dowerless, poor girl like myself over your blind ambition. Or, choosing her, do I not know that your repentance and regret would surely follow if you would have no riches from me to confiscate? I hereby release you from your engagement. I speak these words with a heavy heart, for the love of *him* you once were."

"Spirit! I insist that you remove me from this despicable place. This particular memory that your perverted supernatural magic has been portraying is inflicting upon me great emotional anguish!"

"I told you, you obstinate bonehead, that *these* accurate shadows you are presently witnessing are of the things that have been in the past," the Ghost elaborated and informed. "The events are what they are and were, so do not blame me for what you currently regret!"

"Remove me immediately from this painful overwhelming excruciation!" Scrooge guiltily exclaimed. "I cannot bear it! Leave me! Take me back to my residence. Haunt me no longer, you immortal bastard!"

As Scrooge violently tugged and struggled with the powerful Spirit of Christmas Past, the remorseful time and space traveler became conscious of being physically and emotionally exhausted, and simultaneously, being also overcome by an irresistible drowsiness. And furthermore, the haughty old fool was aware of again being inside his own familiar bed-room. Ebenezer Scrooge had barely scarce time to reel, toss, and turn, before the old fool began sinking into a very deep sleep.

Stave Three
"The Second of the Three Spirits"

Scrooge worriedly awoke inside his dismal upstairs bedroom. There was no doubt about *that* recent, restless, insomnia. His cold feet shuffled into his adjoining sitting-room, and soon the occupant's pupils were distracted by a great light, and the general area had peculiarly undergone an extremely surprising transformation. The walls and ceiling were evidently now hung with living green foliage, and the apartment amazingly resembled a perfect tropical fruit grove. The leaves of holly, mistletoe, and ivy reflected back the light, as if many little mirrors had been scattered about the entire premises.

And such a mighty blaze went roaring-up the much in-need-of-repair chimney, as *that* ancient hearth had never known burning logs in Scrooge's time, or in Jacob Marley's either, or for many and many a winter seasons that had over the years evaporated into history.

Heaped upon the floor, forming a kind of imperial throne, were myriad turkeys, geese, game, ducks, great joints of meat, sucking pigs, long wreaths of sausages, mince-pies, plum-pudding bowls, barrels of oysters, red-hot chestnuts, cherry-cheeked apples, juicy oranges, luscious pears, and immense bowls of savory fruit punch.

Resting comfortably and in an easy state upon this new-found couch sat an illuminated, jovial, green Giant, quite glorious to see, who bore a flaming torch, that in shape, was not unlike Plenty's Horn, and who raised the object high in order to shed its light upon suspicious Scrooge, as the curious, conceited resident came peeping around the doorway.

"Come in; come in! And get to know me better, aged fellow! I am the inimitable Ghost of Christmas Present. Look upon me, you old skinflint! I'll wager a fortune that you've never seen the likes of me before!"

'Holy Angel Shit!' Ebenezer mentally marveled. 'If I were in Jerusalem, this intense vision could be a magnificent Israel-light!'

Then, Scrooge abandoned his ludicrous levity, garnered his distraught senses, and managed to speak to his incredulous guest. "Never before in my long lifetime did my eyes ever witness such a tremendous hoax! Yes, you Fraud. I strongly speculate that you're a colossal mirage; an imaginary aberration or massive hallucination!"

"Have you never before walked forth with the younger members of my family? My esoteric statement meaning, you Ebenezer Scrooge, are an old, over-the-hill fart, and I am very young for my species, even though I'm much more ancient than you happen to be," the inexplicable Phantom nonchalantly remarked.

"I don't think I have had the pleasure of your siblings' acquaintance. I'm afraid that I've never been introduced to any of your trickster kin. Do you have many brothers, Spirit?" Scrooge stuttered, stalling for time to gather his composure. "If so, I believe that they and you must be kindred spirits!"

"Both of your flimsy references are weak and poor attempts at mediocre humor," criticized the Ghost of Christmas Present. "But in honest response to your obvious inferior inquisitiveness, please forgive my abundant chauvinism. Indeed, annually speaking, I've had more than eighteen-hundred brothers since *that* cold night in Bethlehem."

"You said Bethlehem?" an apprehensive Ebenezer Scrooge automatically exclaimed. "I now suspect that you *are* insane, coming to my residence from *bedlam!*"

"You pathetic and absurd dumb fuck!" the aggravated Spirit boomed. "I meant the little town of Bethlehem, situated below Jerusalem in the distant Holy Land, and not that insane local mental asylum, St. Mary of Bethlehem!"

Spiteful Scrooge was suddenly paranoid and nervously ignored the Specter's Biblical and explicit geographic allusions. "You seem to possess a plethora of family members to provide for! Formidable Spirit, cordially conduct me wherever you will. I had recently gone forth with one of your siblings on compulsion, and I had learnt a peculiar ongoing lesson, which is still somewhat working now. To-night, if you have a strong desire to teach me anything worthwhile, then let me profit by it."

"Touch my soft robe and be inspired to accompany my scheduled ramble!" the Ghost of Christmas Present instructed.

Scrooge did as he was told, and his hands held the elaborate green robe tightly. The brilliantly-lit room, along with its contents, all instantly vanished, and the oddball pair *presently* stood within the city streets upon *that* very snowy London Christmas morning.

Baffled Ebenezer and the energetic Ghost meandered ahead, virtually invisible, and traveled effortlessly above the buildings straight to Scrooge's clerk's modest Camden Town rowhome, and on the front door's threshold, the Spirit smiled, and stopped to bless Bob Crotchit's humble dwelling with the casual sprinklings of his potent torch.

Then, up rose Mrs. Edna Crotchit, dressed in a weatherworn gown, adorn in ribbons, which were cheap and made a goodly show for a meager sixpence. And the devoted wife laid the linen tablecloth, assisted in her chores by Belinda, second of her daughters, while Master Peter Crotchit plunged a fork into the saucepan of freshly-peeled potatoes. And now, two smaller Crotchits, a boy and girl, came tearing into the tiny dining room, boisterously screaming that the baker's had successfully smelt the designated table goose, since the family was too poor to afford a traditional holiday turkey meal.

"What has ever got your precious father delayed for dinner?" Mrs. Edna Crotchit asked Belinda. "And your encumbered brother, Tiny Tim! And Martha wasn't as late last Christmas day as she is right now!"

"Here's Martha, mother, now entering our modest house. Please don't hold a vendetta against Martha for being a tad late."

"Here's Martha, mother!" loudly cried and verified the two younger Crotchit daughters. "Hurrah! There's such a goose you're holding! Any later arrival on your part, Martha,"

Belinda emphasized, "and your goose would be cooked. Ha, ha, ha!"

"Why, bless your heart alive, my dear, how late you are?" Mrs. Crotchit greeted, kissing Martha a dozen times, and next taking-off her daughter's shawl and bonnet. "I'm glad that you have a docile personality, Martha." And after closely examining the girl's former headgear, Bob's faithful spouse giggled, "I'm quite happy to report that you don't have a bee in your bonnet!"

"We had a great deal of work to finish-up last night," Martha amiably replied. "And we had to clear-away all the meal preparations early this morning. As you know, mother, Christmas Day comes but once a year, and despite our near poverty home situation, we are quite rich in good health and genuinely blessed with good cheer!"

"It's a good thing that the baker cooking the goose is our relative, your reliable cousin, Davy Crotchit, who doesn't charge us any labor cost, or else, Martha, the goose would've been unaffordable. And it's too bad that we're so poor that we can't afford any of Davy Crotchit's pie alamode for dessert! And Martha, in the past, our baker's sumptuous delicacy was so savory that to this very day, I remember the alamode!"

"Yes, mother. Just take a gander at that exquisite goose on the table! It just gives me goosebumps! Ha, ha, ha!"

"Well! Never mind, so long as you're now warm inside and have escaped the inclement frost, Miss Martha Crotchit. Sit ye down before the fire, my dear, and warm your numb hands. Lord, bless ye, child! After you warm-up some more, we can both bond and chill-out together!"

"No, no! There's father merrily strolling down the lane," Belinda Crotchit disclosed while peering-out the ice-glazed front window.

"Confidentially, Belinda," Mrs. Crotchit stated. "Your father Robert likes to goose my ass every night before he goes to sleep. Your father's obnoxious perversion gives me fabulous goosebumps, just thinking about it!"

"Sounds like Daddy always comes through in the pinch! Ha, Ha, Ha. I've never seen your butt, mother, but I imagine that it must be entirely black and blue! Ha, ha, ha!"

"Hide, Martha, hide! Quick now! Play hide and seek with father!"

So, Martha hid herself behind the shoddy couch, and in came little Bob, with at least three feet of comforter draped down to his knees, exclusive of the frayed fringe. And Bob's threadbare clothes had been carefully darned-up and brushed, to look seasonable. And Tiny Tim was being carried upon his father's shoulders. Alas, for crippled Tiny Tim bore a little crutch of his own, and the lad had his virtually paralyzed limbs supported by sturdy iron frames!

"Why, where's our dear Martha?" cried-out Bob Crotchit, looking around the small dining room.

"Not coming," Mrs. Crotchit replied.

"Not coming!" Bob's voice bellowed, with a sudden declension in his high spirits. "You say *not coming* upon Christmas Day! Then, how did that prepared goose get set upon the table? It's not a turkey that flew over to London from Constantinople! Martha was the one who had been assigned to get the bird from trustworthy Davy Crotchit!"

Martha didn't like seeing her father remaining disappointed, even if it were only in joke or jest. So, the loyal daughter, like an overanxious fetus, came-out prematurely from behind the tattered sofa, and ran into his arms, while the two younger Crotchit daughters admirably hustled Tiny Tim, and bore the lame lad off to the wash-room, so that *he* might delight in hearing his sisters singing "Tip-toe, through the tulips"!

"And how did little Tiny Tim behave?" Mrs. Edna Crotchit inquired, when she had aptly rallied Bob on his credulity, and simultaneously, Bob hugged Martha to his heart's content, nearly squeezing all of the vital oxygen out of the girl's precious lungs.

"As good as gold," Robert exaggerated and described. "And even better. Somehow, Tim gets thoughtful, sitting alone all by himself so much, and the lad thinks and speaks the strangest things you've ever heard. Our son told me, coming home, that he hoped that the people saw him while we were in the church, because he was a cripple, and it might be pleasant to them to remember, upon Christmas Day, exactly *Who* made lame beggars walk and made blind men see. Those who had observed Tiny Tim in church right away would easily understand that Jesus, in later life, would whip-up miracles!"

Bob's voice was tremulous when he related *that* graphic and impactful information to his family, and his hands quivered even more when Crotchit informed his wife and children that he believed Tiny Tim was growing stronger with every passing day.

The afflicted boy's little crutch was soon heard upon the planked floor, and back came Tiny Tim before another word could be uttered, escorted by his protective sisters to his stool (here, not feces), situated beside the stone fireplace. And while Bob, turning-up his frayed cuffs, as if, poor fellow, they were capable of being made even more shabby, the family patriarch compounded some hot mixture inside a jug with diluted gin and lemon juice, and then vigorously stirred the ingredients around and around, quickly placing the mixture upon the hob to gradually simmer. Master Peter and the two ubiquitous younger Crotchit girls ambled over to fetch the mashed potatoes, with which they soon returned in high procession.

"It's too bad that our goose isn't the talented one in fairy tales that could lay the fabulous golden eggs," Bob very facetiously regretted. "Even my wildly strange employer Ebenezer Scrooge couldn't afford to own such a talented, fabled bird. Just yesterday, the old merchant made a slip of the tongue and accidentally called me Bob Crotch-shit! Ha, ha, ha! What a miserly ham that miserable turkey is! Ha, ha, ha!"

Mrs. Edna Crotchit had prepared the gravy (ready beforehand in a tiny saucepan) that was absolutely hissing hot; Master Peter mashed and smashed the potatoes with incredible vigor; Miss Belinda skillfully sweetened-up the delicious apple-sauce; Martha dusted the hot plates; Bob lifted and took Tiny Tim beside him to a small corner at the table; the two young Cratchit girls set chairs for everybody, not forgetting themselves, and mounting guard upon their posts, crammed spoons into their mouths, lest the famished twosome should shrick for delectable goose before their turn.

At last, the dishes were set upon the table, and grace was officially and piously prayed by the whole family. The solemn utterance was succeeded by a breathless pause, as Mrs. Crotchit, gazing slowly and feeling all along the carving-knife, plunged the weapon into the goose's tender breast. But when the wife did so, and when the long-expected gush of stuffing issued forth, one murmur of delight arose all around the board, and even normally reticent Tiny Tim, beat upon the table with the handle of his knife, and feebly cried, "Merry Christmas", as if he were a starving little drummer boy!

There never was such a mediocre goose as the one that had been placed upon the table. Bob insisted with rhetorical hyperbole that he didn't believe there ever was such a "marvelous goose" cooked in any expensive restaurant kitchen throughout the entire city. Its tenderness, flavor, size, and cheapness were all that the family's meager budget could afford. Eked-out by apple-sauce and mashed potatoes, the entire feast was a sufficient and adequate dinner for the whole convivial family to enjoy.

Indeed, as Mrs. Crotchit maintained *that* steadfast oral banter with great delight, her keen eyes were surveying any evidence of meat upon any small bone remaining on anyone's empty dish. Yet everyone seated had finally had enough holiday sustenance, and the youngest Crotchits in particular, were steeped in cranberry sauce and sweet onion to the eyebrows! But now, the plates were being changed by Miss Belinda, and Mrs. Crotchit swiftly left the room, and putting it mildly, to take the dessert pudding to the table, and with urgent dispatch, carrying the family's favorite snack from the kitchen into the dining area.

Being highly motivated by impromptu comedy, facetious Bob Crotchit immediately poured a pint of cheap whiskey into the pudding, and mercilessly hollered-out, "The proof is in the pudding! Ha, ha, ha! Oh, such a wonderful pudding," Bob loudly yelled, indicating that he regarded the served dessert as the greatest culinary success ever achieved by Mrs. Crotchit ever since their very ordinary wedding reception. The cozy scene was now abundantly apparent that the Camden Town Crotchits wholeheartedly believed in the splendid credo, "Little things mean a lot"!

At last, the tasty dinner meal had been fully consumed, the tablecloth was cleared, the hearth swept, and the fire's flames accelerated with additional wood. After the compound mixed in the brandy jug had been sampled, tasted, and considered perfect, ripe apples were set upon the table, and a shovelful of chestnuts were roasted on the open fire.

Then, all the Crotchit family drew around the hearth, in what Bob called a "square-circle", and considerate Robert diplomatically proposed a most wonderful toast. "A Merry Christmas to us all, my dears. God bless us!"

Which all the family re-echoed in unison, "Yes, God bless us every one!" Promptly, handicapped Tiny Tim, showing innocent consent, candidly verified and wholeheartedly reiterated the group response.

The happy lad sat very close to his father's side, mounted upon his little stool. Bob held the boy's withered little hand in his, symbolizing that *his* heart completely loved the physically impaired child, and the father wished to keep Tim by his side, and dreaded that the young boy might be taken by fate's decree from *his* dedicated, protective care.

Scrooge speedily raised his head, on soon hearing his own name being addressed. "And yes, let us not forget my employer, Mr. Scrooge," Bob loudly proclaimed. "I'll give you a toast, Mr. Ebenezer Scrooge, the benevolent Founder of the current Feast, *our*

Christmas Feast! Thank you for giving me my wonderful clerk's job!"

"The Founder of the Feast, indeed!" Mrs. Edna Crotchit vehemently objected with a reddened face. "I wish I had *him* here right this minute! I'd give that callous humbug the dickens, along with a nasty piece of my mind to feast upon, and I hope he'd have a good appetite choking on it. I believe that soon the Devil will claim *your pretend uncle's* corrupt soul as *his* exclusive property!"

"My dear," Robert cautiously maintained. "Watch what your lips utter in front of the children. Kindly respect our children's pure innocence! Especially on Christmas Day."

"It should be Christmas Day, I am sure," Edna Crotchit agreed and confirmed with a degree of disdain, "on which one drinks to the health of such an odious, stingy, hard, unfeeling man as cruel Mr. Ebenezer Scrooge happens to be. You know, husband, that *your* contemptible employer is quite a heinous human charlatan. Yes, Robert! Nobody knows it better than you do, you obedient wimp!"

"My dear Edna," Bob mildly answered. "On this splendid morning, ample kindness should abound throughout the entire city! It's Christmas Day."

"I'll reluctantly drink to the old coot's health, simply for *your* sake, and with *us* honoring the day's religious significance," Edna cynically replied. "But not solely for *his* friggin' sake. Long life to him, you say! A Merry Christmas and a Happy New Year! He'll be very merry and happy about counting his gold coins, and being lustfully alone inside his reclusive existence; I have no doubt, the loveless hermit!"

The quiet children swallowed-down their separate toasts after hearing Edna's critical commentary. It was the first of their dinner proceedings which had no detectable family unity abounding in it. Tiny Tim drank his toast last of all, but the youngster didn't care one iota about either alcohol or Mr. Ebenezer Scrooge, whom the boy hardly knew. The old fart was, without a doubt, the principal ogre of the family's many remote acquaintances. The mention of *his* loathsome name had instantaneously cast a dark shadow upon the party participants; indeed, a lingering, sour feeling which was not thoroughly dispelled for a full five minutes.

The general atmosphere eventually then transformed and became exceedingly merrier than before, resulting from the mere relief of "Scrooge the Baleful" being fully dispensed with. Bob Crotchit told the gathering how he had a situation in his eye for Master Peter's intended employment at Scrooge's despised accounting firm, which would bring in, if obtained, a full three pounds and sixpence weekly. The two young Crotchits girls laughed tremendously at the weird idea of Peter ever being a man of business, while Peter's peter instantaneously pricked-up upon the prospect of him entering adulthood, and finally earning a job that provided a lowly pauper's salary.

There was nothing of a high mark prevalent within the family conversation. The Crotchits were not a handsome family in terms of economic stability; were not well-dressed; and their tarnished shoes were far from being water-proof; their clothes were scanty; and Peter might have known, and very likely did, the inside of a pawnbroker's shop, that would be desperately needed to temporarily borrow money in order to, at times, make financial ends meet.

But despite the clan's monetary adversity, the Crotchits were happy, grateful, quite pleased with one another's company, and rather contented with the difficult 'money time' during *that* jubilant Christmas Day. And when the visiting Spirit's torch still touched the family's hearts at parting, Scrooge had his eye upon the poor-but-gleeful group, and especially focused his undivided attention upon thankful Tiny Tim.

It was a great surprise to Scrooge, as *that* most-impactful scene vanished from his view, to hear a heavy and forceful laugh. It was a much greater surprise to Scrooge to recognize the distinct guffaw as his own nephew's joviality, and to soon find himself standing inside a bright, dry, gleaming room, with the enthralled Spirit standing and smiling by *his* side, and looking at that same nephew present and actively celebrating Christmas in a more opulent and genteel home environment.

While there is infection in disease and sorrow, there is nothing in the world so irresistibly contagious as laughter and good-humor among congenial associates, friends and family. When Scrooge's jolly nephew prodigeously laughed, Scrooge's niece by marriage laughed as hardily as he. And *their* acquaintances, being not a bit inhibited, laughed hardily in harmonious compliance.

"Uncle Scrooge often stressed to me that Christmas was a humbug, as sure as I live!" Scrooge's nephew recollected and verbally shared. "Regretfully, my rich relative actually believed his disgusting bullshit, too!"

"More shame for him, Fred!" Scrooge's niece-by-marriage instantly affirmed rather indignantly. "Your deplorable uncle hasn't enough grace to even be a veritable disgrace! *Your* grumpy Uncle Ebenezer is partly hypocritical, partly sarcastic, and wholly nasty in temperament!"

"Indeed, Mildred. Bob Cratchit had told me that last week several businessmen from the Exchange came by my uncle's dilapidated accounting house, politely asking for generous donations to the poor. Volatile Uncle Scrooge then caustically admonished the gentlemen's volunteer charity work by telling the fine and decent local merchants to get their silly clown show the hell out of his office! Uncle Ebenezer's intolerant attitude was extremely embarrassing!"

Fred's wife Mildred was very pretty; yes, exceedingly attractive. With a dimpled face, the young lady possessed a surprised-looking, yes, capital visage; a ripe little mouth that seemed made to be kissed, as no doubt it often was; all kinds of entrancing little dots formed about her chin, tiny spots that melted into one another when she incessantly smiled.

And adorable Mildred featured the sunniest pair of eyes you ever saw being sported upon any gorgeous feminine creature's face.

Altogether, Fred's gorgeous soulmate was what an astute observer would have described as being a provocative female, but conversely, behaving majorly satisfactory, also. Oh, just how perfectly satisfactory.

"He's just a comical-but-eccentric old fellow," Mr. Scrooge's fair-minded nephew objectively filibustered. "That's the honest-to-goodness truth; and the insecure ogre's not so pleasant as he might or should be. However, his verbal offenses and myriad insults carry their own punishment, and I have nothing negative to say against him, for final judgment will be the Lord's singular responsibility. Tell me, now; who actually suffers by *his* ill whims? He himself, and always. Here, the dysfunctional old skeptic takes it into his head to intentionally dislike us, and Uncle Scrooge won't come and dine with us. What's the immediate consequence? The maniac only loses a festive dinner, and despite his nastiness, the elderly coin-counter possesses a rather feeble appetite to boot."

"Indeed, I think he loses a very good dinner along with plenty of quality merriment," Scrooge's opinionated niece-by-marriage contributed to the discussion. Everybody else in attendance affirmed the same basic evaluation, and the holiday guests must have been competent judges, because the separate revelers had just enjoyed a fine turkey dinner; and, with the expensive cake dessert upon the table, the attendees were clustered round the fire, sharing sundry anecdotes by lamplight.

"Well, I'm very glad to hear it," Scrooge's nephew smiled and stated. "Because I haven't any great faith in today's cynics that are quite prevalent all over London Town. What do you say about my uncle's demeanor, Topper?"

Topper clearly had his eyes that had been keenly focused upon one of Scrooge's niece's sisters, for Fred's friend wisely answered that a visiting bachelor was a wretched outcast, who had "no right" to express an opinion on the sensitive family subject. Scrooge's niece's plump-and-busty sister blushed at hearing Topper's general-but-sagacious evaluation.

After tea had been served, the garrulous group sang several popular Christmas carols, for the assembled company was a musical assortment of gay and straight friends, and the eclectic entourage deliberately sang in a totally dissonant manner a conventional Glee tune. Especially embarked on-a-courting-mission, Topper, who could growl-away in his natural bass voice like a good and faithful hunting hound, and who never swelled the large veins in his neck and forehead during his singing endeavor, or got red in the face over it, even when sporting a decent erection while staring at Scrooge's voluptuous niece's younger-but-bustier plump sister.

But the assemblage at Fred's fairly luxurious townhouse didn't devote the whole evening to singing and satirizing seasonal music. After a while, the friends played at forfeits; for it is good to behave like dumb-ass children sometimes, and never better than at Christmas, when its mighty Founder had been a manger child, wrapped in swaddling clothes.

There was next a game at blind-man's-buff, even though some of the participants were female. And it was plainly evident that preoccupied Topper was really captivated having both of his wandering eyes and throbbing testicles concentrated on his well-endowed female objective. Knocking down the fire-irons, tumbling over the well-upholstered chairs, bumping up against the piano, smothering himself among the curtains, wherever Fred's niece's chubby sister meandered, Topper's massive, stiff hard-on followed like a pulsating weather vane! The horny asshole always knew exactly where the obese sister was prancing and gallivanting.

"Here is a new game," Scrooge suggested to his amiable Spirit companion. "One half-hour, Spirit, only one half-hour more to remain in this contagious, blithe environment!"

"What game, you old devil? Instead, Mr. Skinflint; let us secretly eavesdrop on your nephew's novel inspiration!"

In a Challenging Game called "Yes and No", Scrooge's jovial nephew had to think of something innovative, and the rest of the attendees were directed to question and find-out precisely what Fred was contemplating; the designated clues being that perhaps the secret subject was an animal, yes, a live animal, that was rather a disagreeable animal, yes, sometimes a savage animal; an animal that growled and grunted at times, and talked sometimes, and that lived a lonely life in polluted London, and walked about the streets like a mendicant, and wasn't made a show of, and wasn't led by anybody, and didn't live in a menagerie or in a zoo, and was never killed in a crowded market; and was not a horse, or a donkey, or a cow, or a bull, or a tiger, or a dog, or a pig, or a cat, or a bear.

At every new question put to him, Fred, Scrooge's most valued employee, burst into a fresh roar of stellar laughter, and was so inexpressibly tickled that the amused nephew was obliged to get-up off the sofa and stamp his feet in absolute delight. At last, the plump sister, or Topper's main pursuit, cried-out, "I have found-out the great mystery! I know what it is you're cleverly describing!"

"What is it, then?" Fred shrieked, nearly swallowing his tonsils.

"The secret animal is your reprehensible Uncle Scro-o-o-ge!"

At that singular moment, Scrooge had imperceptibly become so gay and light of heart, that he felt like drinking a toast showing his full approval. But the whole scene slowly passed-off and vaporized in the breath of the last words spoken by his only nephew, and a suddenly depressed Ebenezer, along with the accommodating Spirit, were again embarked upon their urban travels.

Much truth the itinerant pair had seen, and over far distances the two had ventured, and many homes the strange companions had scurried by, but always with a happy ending. The Spirit and Scrooge currently stood beside sick-beds, and the horizontal occupants lying in the hospital ward were cheerful, despite their individual maladies. Next, the two flying travelers astonishingly journeyed to foreign lands, and somehow, were again magically close at home in London; the duo zoomed by laboring men, and next sped by abject poverty, and the abominable curse was represented, somehow, as a rich and rewarding experience.

Inside an almshouse, in a hospital clinic, and also inside a jail, the pair was constantly speeding-along, halting in misery's every refuge, where vain mankind, in his little brief authority, had not made fast the door, and those in power had not intentionally barred-out the mirthful Spirit of Christmas Past. The Arcane Specter mercifully left his benign blessing, and had voluntarily taught and demonstrated to melancholy Scrooge *his* constructive guiding precepts, along with his magnificent wisdom. Suddenly, as the time and space travelers stood together in an open place, the familiar distant church bell tolled.

Scrooge thoroughly looked-about his surroundings for signs of the departing benign Ghost of Christmas Present, and noticed its incredible two-dimensional form no more. As the last stroke of the tower clock ceased vibrating, apprehensive Ebenezer remembered the audacious prediction of old Jacob Marley, and, lifting-up his weary eyes, beheld a silent, dark Phantom, draped and hooded, advancing like a heavy mist along the frozen ground, engaged in an awesome, dreadful approach.

Stave Four
"The Last of the Three Spirits"

The fearsome Phantom slowly, gravely, and silently drifted forward. When the morbid figure arrived near his presence, Scrooge bent-down upon his knee in apparent supplication; for the air through which that gruesome Spirit moved seemed to turbulently scatter ethereal gloom and mystery in all directions.

The ghoulish apparition was shrouded in a deep black garment, which concealed its head, its face, its form, and left nothing of itself visible save one gruesome, outstretched, bony hand. Being apprehensive and greatly frightened, Scrooge knew only awe, for the horrible Spirit neither spoke nor moved.

"I am in the presence of the Ghost of Christmas Yet to Come? Ghost of the Future! I cower to you more than any fantastic specter I have yet encountered. But as I know your salient purpose is to do me good, and as I hope to live to be another man from what I had been, I'm quite prepared to bear you company, and do it with a thankful heart. Will you not speak to me?"

The prodigious ghost gave his new-found ward no verbal reply. The grotesque-looking stiff hand was pointed straight before Scrooge's scrutiny.

"Are you sent by divine intervention, or are you on some secular occult visitation? Oh well, I suppose that my inquisitiveness is irrelevant at the moment. Lead on, then! Lead on Wretched Spirit! The night is waning fast, and there is precious time left for me to redeem myself. I know that my remaining future is both dim and limited in both scope and sequence. I beg you! Please lead on, Spirit!"

The duo seemed to swiftly enter the city proper, for the metropolis, although it was officially winter, seemed to rather spring-up about their wandering. But there the pair appeared, stationed in the heart of London; on

'Change', the Exchange being a thoroughly active scene of preoccupied daily merchants.

The very awesome Morose Spirit, akin in physical appearance to the fabled Grim Reaper, stopped beside one small knot of conversing business-men. Observing that the terrible hand was pointed toward the huddle, Scrooge advanced closer to readily eavesdrop on their whispered dialogue.

"No," said a great fat man with a monstrous chin. "I don't know much about it, either way. I only know from reliable sources that the greedy son-of-a-bitch is dead."

"When did the insufferable miser die?" curiously inquired a second merchant, standing bent-over in the busy noontime square.

"Last night, I believe. In his sleep!"

"Why, what was the matter with him? I thought that the diabolical scumbag would never die."

"God only knows," the first self-important commerce tycoon added, followed with a rather healthy, rather-unconcerned yawn.

"What has *he* done with his money? With his amassed fortune?" a red-faced gentleman then asked.

"I yet haven't heard any gossip," the importer with the enlarged jaw related. "Company has retained his majority stock holdings, perhaps. He hasn't left any of it to me. That's all the fuck I know. Bye-bye!"

Scrooge was at first inclined to be surprised that the Spirit should attach any particular significance to a casual conversation that seemed so apparently trivial. But feeling assured that it must have some important hidden purpose, the narrow-minded bonehead set himself to consider what the dialogue was likely to be. It could scarcely be supposed to have any bearing on the death of Jacob Marley, his old petulant partner, who positively despised his younger brother Roberto's uncanny version of Jamaican music, for *that* small funeral had occurred seven years in the Past, and this Ghost's distinct province was the unforeseen Future.

Scrooge curiously looked-about in that very familiar place for his own image; but another man, a total stranger, stood in *his* accustomed corner, and although the clock pointed to his usual time of day for being there, the old skinflint noticed no likeness of himself amongst the multitude that poured into the city's main market-house through "the Porch". The vision afforded the elderly, scrupulous observer little surprise, however, for Ebenezer had been assessing in his convoluted mind a certain change of attitude, and the truth contemplator thought and hoped he would perceive his new-born resolutions carried-out in *that* new-found manifestation.

The Spirit and its assigned human ward left that rather hectic scene, and astoundingly flew-off into an obscure section of the city, arriving at a low shop where an eclectic array of iron, old rags, bottles, bones, and greasy offal were bought, bartered, or discarded. A gray-haired rascal, of great age, patiently sat upon an abandoned wine barrel, diligently smoking his pipe.

Scrooge and the fully-laconic Phantom inexplicitly came into the presence of *that* idle vagabond bloke, just as a hoary bitch carrying a heavy bundle awkwardly rushed into the alley. But the scrubwoman had scarcely arrived, when another wrinkle-faced female, similarly shabbily laden, made her unplanned rendezvous, too; and the second woman was closely followed by a sinister-looking man, totally clad in faded black. After a short period of blank astonishment, in which the old bearded fellow with the abbreviated pipe had eagerly joined the assembled trio, the four all coincidentally burst into a thunderous roar.

"Let the impetuous charwoman alone to be the first!" suggested the same retired whore who had arrived second. "Let myself, a mere laundress alone to be the second sorter; and allow the undertaker's morbid assistant alone to be the third. Look here, old Joe. Here's an opportune chance! If we haven't all four met here at the same time, without actually intending it, I conjecture that our impromptu meeting has truly been dictated by fate!"

Fifteen minute later, a second conversation ensued outside the location. "You couldn't have met me in a better place. You were made free of it long ago, you know; and the other two rummagers ain't exactly strangers, either," Joe theorized and uttered. "What have you got to sell, Mrs. Dilber? What have you got to sell from your recent acquisitions?"

"Half a minute's patience, Joe, and you shall see my body, er, I mean, my recently pilfered booty."

"What odds then! What odds, Mrs. Dilber?" the impatient second woman wondered and asked so that she could sell her recently purloined items for cash. "Every person has a right to take care of themselves. *He* always did! Who's the worse for the loss of a few expensive articles like these gems? Not a dead man, I suppose."

Mrs. Dilber, whose present glib manner was remarkable for general propitiation, casually answered, "No, indeed, ma'am. That cheap conniver Mr. Scrooge is as dead as Moses and Julius Caesar, that he is. The old miser never did change his self-centered, aberrent ways!"

"If the malevolent asshole wanted to keep his property for beneficiaries after he was dead, the wicked old screw, why wasn't he natural in his lifetime? If he had been a decent human being, he'd have had somebody to look after and care for his possessions when he was struck with Death, instead of him lying alone, gasping-out his last breath inside his bed, all terribly isolated by himself."

"It's the truest verdict that ever was spoken, in the Bible or otherwise, Joe confidently asserted. "It's an authentic judgment on him that you've just described."

"I wish it was a little heavier judgment, and it definitely should've been, you may depend upon it," Mrs. Dilber communicated. "If I could've laid my hands on anything else, I would've quickly acted without any guilt. Open that bundle, old Joe, and let me know the value of it. Speak-out plain and clear. I'm not afraid to be the first benefactor, nor afraid for his anonymous heirs to see my prizes."

Huckster Joe went-down upon his knees for the greater convenience of opening the bundle, and his initial inspection dragged-out a large and heavy roll of some dark material.

"What do you call this dusty fabric? Bed-curtains, I believe! Ah! Yes! Bed-curtains, most certainly! Don't drop that messy oil upon the blankets, now." cautioned gray-haired Joe.

"His blankets, pillows and sheets?" Mrs. Templeton, the impulsive second lady asked.

"Whose else's do you think? Deceased Mr. Scrooge isn't likely to take cold without 'em, I dare say." Mrs. Dilber claimed. "Ah, a bonus! You may look through *that* exquisite shirt till your eyes ache; but you won't find a tiny hole in it; nor a threadbare place. It's the best attire he had, and a fine piece of apparel, too. The mortician would've wasted *my* trophy by dressing the louse up in it for *his* impending wake, if it hadn't been for me first confiscatin' it. I must admit that this activity is *our* own *undertaking,* ha, ha, ha!"

Scrooge intently listened to the hideous conversation in incredulous horror. "Spirit! I see, I now fully see. The case of this unhappy man might be parallel to my own. My life tends to move in a similar way, now. Merciful Heaven, what unfathomable bullshit is this that I'm now witnessing!"

The surrounding scene had drastically changed, and now Ebenezer Scrooge's right hand almost touched a bare, un-curtained bed. A pale ethereal light, rising from the planked floor up into the ceiling, deflected straight-down upon the designated bed. And upon its unraveled spread, unwatched, unwept upon, uncared for, lay the deceased body of a withered, plundered, unknown man.

"Spirit, let me see some tenderness associated with a despicable death, or else, this dark chamber, you Unholy Ghost, will be forever present, haunting my perplexed mind and soul directly into obscure infinity."

The ghastly Ghost Guide next adroitly conducted Scrooge to poor Bob Crotchit's Camden Town rowhouse, the precise humble dwelling which the cantankerous penny-pincher had recently visited before, and *his* visual investigation found the mother and the children sadly seated around the ineffective fireplace.

Quiet. Very quiet. The noisy little Crotchits were as still as statues in one corner, and the gathered contingent sat looking-up at Peter, who had a sacred prayer book held before his eyes. The pensive mother and her despondent daughters were quietly engaged in doing needle-work. But surely, the family members were all very distraught and disconsolate!

"And he took a child, and set him in the midst of them," Peter Crotchit verbally read and sobbed.

Where had Scrooge heard those prophetic words before? Quite obviously, the regretful scoundrel had not currently dreamed the now-familiar nomenclature. The saddened boy must have possibly read them aloud a first time, as Ebenezer and the illustrious Spirit of Christmas Future had deftly crossed the threshold into the humble home.

The mother laid her needlework upon the small wooden table, and demonstrating her mounting grief, put her hand up to her face and strongly wept.

"The color hurts my eyes," Edna Crotchit commented to disguise the reason for her tears.

"The color? Ah, poor Tiny Tim!" Martha contributed and sobbed.

"They're better now, again. The fire glow makes my eyes weak by candle-light, and I wouldn't show weak eyes to your father when he comes home, for the world. It must be near *his* arrival time."

"Past it, rather, Mother," Peter answered, silently shutting-up his religious book. "But I think he has walked a little slower than he used to amble, these last few evenings, anyway."

"I have known him to proudly walk with," Edna Crotchit whimpered and then resumed her melancholy speech. "I have known him proudly to walk with Tiny Tim upon his shoulder, at times, very fast indeed."

"And so have I," Peter verified. "Often."

"And so have I!" exclaimed another. And so had all.

"But Tiny Tim *was* very light to carry, and his father loved him so, that it was no trouble, no trouble whatsoever," Mrs. Edna Crotchit expressed. "And there is your father now, arriving at the front door!"

The devoted wife hurried-out to meet her financially unsuccessful husband; and little Bob in his comforter, for he had desperate need of it, poor fellow, eagerly stepped inside. His tea was ready for his consumption upon the hob, and the sorrowed children all competed as to who should help him to it first. Then, the two young Crotchit girls got upon his knees and laid, each child, a little cheek against his face, as if the daughters symbolically expressed, "Don't mind it, father. Please don't be grieved!"

Despite his overall sadness, Bob was philosophically cheerful, and spoke pleasantly to all his family. Crotchit looked at the accumulated needlework heaped upon the table, and praised the domestic industry and speed of Mrs. Crotchit and their helpful daughters.

"Sunday! You went to-day, then, Robert?" Edna inquired. "I'm so dejected that I couldn't endure such enormous mental depression as you have just had."

"Yes, my dear," Bob politely returned. "Please don't be inconsolable! I only wish you could've gone and accompanied me to the cemetery. It would've done you good to see how green and inspirational a place it is. But I predict that you'll wish to see it often. I had promised Tiny Tim that I would walk there each and every Sunday to honor his short life. My little child! My little, little child!"

Robert broke-down all at once. The father couldn't thwart or stifle his emotional reaction. The modest home was as silent as the funeral director's empty grieving parlor.

"Specter," Scrooge acknowledged and mentioned. "Something informs me that our parting moment is at hand. I know it, but I know not how. Tell me now; what man that was, with the covered face, whom we saw lying quite dead inside his curtained bed?"

The ominous Ghost of Christmas Yet to Come conveyed his troubled ward to a dismal, wretched, ruinous churchyard. The daunting Spirit stood among the graves, and pointed-down to *One* headstone in particular.

"Macabre Spirit. I can't believe that people are dying to get into this horrendous place. Before I draw nearer to that stone to which you point, answer me one vital question," Scrooge urgently urged. "Are these the shadows of the things that Will Be, or are they merely the shadows of the things that May Be Only?"

Still, the enigmatic, sinister Ghost pointed downward to the weed-laden, unkempt grave by which it and its human companion stood.

"Men's courses will foreshadow certain ends, to which, if persevered in, they must lead. But if the courses be departed from, the ends will most definitely change," Scrooge sincerely declared. "Say it is thus with what you presently show me!"

The reticent Spirit was immovable as ever, and continued pointing downward at the faded grimy gravestone.

Scrooge crept on his knees towards the burial marker, trembling as his deliberate crawling advanced. And, with his fatigued eyes following his arthritic index finger, the elderly gent's pupils read upon the stone of the neglected grave his own despised name, EBENEZER SCROOGE.

"Am I that unfortunate man who lay upon the recently observed death bed? No, Spirit! Oh no, no! Spirit! Hear my dire plea! I am not the man I was. I will not be the man I must have been, but for our extraordinary non-sexual intercourse," greatly distressed Scrooge confessed. "Why show me this contemptible scenario, if I am presently past all hope? Assure me that I may yet change these shadows you've explicitly shown me, by me gratefully organizing an altered life in the brief time I have left."

For the first time, the old fogey's repugnant hand faltered, and his formerly conceited will conceded to essential truth. "I pledge I'll honor Christmas in my heart, and try keeping its message all the year. I will gladly live in the Past, in the Present, and in the Future. The marvelous Spirits of all three shall strive and thrive within my being. I'll not shut-out the important lessons that they teach. Oh, tell me my impending destiny, so that I may sponge-away the condemned writing etched onto this detestable stone!"

The Death Spirit felt compelled to speak in a haunting bass voice. "Yes, for you see, Ebenezer, your nephew Fred, along with your loyal employee, Robert Crotchit, have already died in *this* prospective vision of the Future. Both had loyally taken care of your grave, but over time, even *their* cemetery plots have become weed-infested."

"Dear Fred would have kept my grave in fine condition, and Bob, with his trusty sponge, would've assisted my loyal nephew in performing his endeavor."

Holding-up his hands in one last prayer, specifically designed to have his horrendous fate reversed, a reformed Ebenezer Scrooge noticed an alteration in the Phantom's black hood and cloak. The morose guide shrunk-down, collapsed, and quite instantaneously. dwindled into an ordinary bedpost.

Yes, and the alluded-to vertical bedpost was indeed *his* very own. The bed was his own, and the drab room was also his own. Best and happiest of all, the Time remaining before him was indeed his own; yes, a most propitious interval, in which his conscience could make necessary amends!

Scrooge's astute awareness of his present surroundings was distracted by the city churches ringing-out the lustiest and most powerful peals his ears had ever heard. Running to the overhead window, the changed fellow forcefully opened it, and instantly put-out his hoary head. No fog, no mist, no night; yes, a clear, bright, stirring, golden morning.

"What's today?" Scrooge screamed below, calling downward to a shocked neighborhood boy clad in handsome Sunday clothes, who perhaps had been loitering and naughtily skipping Sunday school attendance.

"Eh?" the confused young wanderer replied, looking-up in astonishment.

"What's today, my fine young fellow?"

"Today! Have you just returned from Mars or Jupiter? Why, today is CHRISTMAS."

"It's Christmas Day! I haven't missed it. I say hallo, down there, my fine freckle-faced fellow! Can you hear my words?"

"Hallo up there! You insane, old fool!"

"Do you know the paltry Poulterer's Place, in the next street but one, located at the busy corner?"

"I should hope I do. I don't suffer from amnesia like you do!"

"An intelligent boy! A remarkable boy! A wonderful smart-ass destined to grow into a genuine wise-ass! Do you' know whether they've sold the prize Turkey that had been hanging up there yesterday? Not the little prize Turkey, mind you, but the much bigger one?"

"What, the one that's as big as me?"

"What a delightful boy! It's a pure pleasure simply to speak with him. Yes, my buck! Let's now talk turkey, gobble, gobble, gobble! Ha, ha, ha!"

"It's hanging there now, Mr. Scrooge."

"Is it? Well, then go and immediately buy and fetch it for me."

"WALK-er!" exclaimed the rattled boy. "Yes, old man! I think you need a walker, or perhaps a wobbly, used, obsolete wheelchair!"

"No, no, you little smart-ass! I am in earnest. Go and buy it, and tell 'em to bring it here to my infamous residence, so that I may give the delivery man the exact direction as to where to deliver the enormous bird. Come back with the owner, whom I know, and I'll give you a shilling. Come back with Mr. Hawkins in less than five-minutes, and I'll gladly give you half a crown!"

The motivated boy, almost pissing his Sunday pants, was off like a pistol shot in the direction of the local merchant's butcher shop.

"I'll send the prize turkey directly to Bob Crotchit's place over in Camden Town! He shan't know who sends it. It's twice the size of Tiny Tim. Joe Hawkins never participated in such a joke as me sending it to Bob's shabby shanty, will be! The unsuspecting family will be absolutely euphoric!"

The hand in which Scrooge scribbled the specific address was not a steady one; but enthusiastically jotting-down the special details, the bizarre fellow somehow did, and the reformed old goat carelessly rambled downstairs to open the street door, ready for the coming of the contacted poulterer.

It was a fantastic, gigantic Turkey, indeed! The oversized bird never could have stood upon his legs, let alone fly five-feet into the air. The fowl would have snapped its skinny appendages off in a minute, like brittle sticks of sealing-wax.

Scrooge dressed himself all in his best finery, and at last maneuvered his blithe body, hilariously meandering out into the street. The crowd of people was by that time pouring forth, just as the new pedestrian had seen the area residents wandering about as *he* had previously witnessed with the help of the Ghost of Christmas Present.

And, merrily strolling with his hands cupped behind his hunched back, Scrooge regarded every one his person confronted with a delightful smile. His visage appeared so irresistibly pleasant, in a word, that three or four good-humored gentlemen and their ladies actually announced, "Good morning, sir! A Merry Christmas to you!" And Scrooge often divulged afterwards, that of all the happy sounds he had ever heard, those were the most sensational to ever enter his ears.

In the afternoon, Ebenezer turned his street path towards his nephew's upscale center city townhouse. The old geezer had indecisively passed the door a dozen times, before the wealthy chap managed to amass sufficient courage to clamber-up the marble steps and softly knock.

"Is your master at home, my dear?" Scrooge requested of the cute, petite girl answering the door. 'Nice girl! Very courteous and mannerly.'

"Yes, sir."

"Where is he, my love?"

"He's probably taking a dump in his favorite pot, but I believe he'll soon be in the dining-room, sir, with his Mistress."

"Master Frederick knows me especially well," Scrooge elaborated, with his hand already firmly positioned upon the entrance knob. "I'll go inside and wait for his arrival, my dear."

"Why, bless my soul!" Fred exclaimed. "Who's that?"

"It's I. Your nefarious and heinous Uncle Scrooge. I've finally accepted your cordial invitation to come to dinner. Will you let me stay, Nephew?"

It is a celestial mercy that Scrooge didn't flamboyantly shake Fred's arm off. The old codger felt quite welcome and at home in five short minutes. Ebenezer's comely niece-by-marriage looked just the same as she had when Scrooge had been accompanied to the residence by the Ghost of Christmas Present. So did Topper, when the horny suitor later arrived. So did the plump sister with the gargantuan breasts, when she came to be lustfully pursued and courted. So did everyone else when the invitees eventually gaily entered Fred's well-furnished abode. Wonderful party, wonderful games, wonderful unanimity, wonder-ful happiness!

But coy Ebenezer was early inside his all-too-familiar dull office next morning. Oh, the shrewd conniver was on the scene so especially early. If the workaholic could only be there first, and catch Bob Crotchit coming-inside the front portal late! That was the irresistible prospect which cagey "Uncle Scrooge" had set his scheming heart upon.

And the elderly schemer actually had accomplished his prime objective. The office clock struck nine, but there was no sign of tardy Bob. A quarter past. No Bob. In fact, Crotchit was a full eighteen and a half minutes dilatory. Scrooge sat laughing to himself with his door wide open, so that the sly business proprietor might easily observe his craven employee come late into *his* subordinate tank.

Bob's hat was off, before the neurotic clerk ever attempted to close the door, along with his dangling comforter, too. Immediately, the worried employee was assiduously laboring upon his stool in a jiffy, and in a frenzy, driving-away with his quill pen, as if he were a possessed, crazed maniac wildly trying to aggressively overtake his nine o'clock delay.

"Hallo!" Scrooge growled like a savage grizzly bear, exercising his accustomed hoarse voice, as near as his voice-box could ineloquently feign. "What do you mean, sir, by coming in here at this rather disappointing time of day?"

"I'm very sorry, sir. I apologize that I am behind my time. I promise to compensate for my regrettable mistake by staying overtime."

"You are? Yes. I think you are. Step this way, laddy, 'as you like it', to quote William Shakespeare, if you please."

"It's only once a year, sir. I assure you that it shall not be repeated, I do swear on a stack of Korans, er, I mean Bibles. I was making rather merry yesterday, sir."

"Now, I'll tell you what, my lethargic friend. I'm not going to stand for this sort of habitual irresponsibility any longer. And therefore, Master Robert," Scrooge continued his admonishment in a fake, angry tone, leaping like an obsessed frog from his stool, and then giving Bob such a dig in the waistcoat that the alarmed recipient staggered back into the tank. "And therefore, Master Robert, I am about to substantially raise your puny salary!"

Bob Crotchit trembled upon his rickety stool, and promptly, his lowered head became a little nearer to the desk's ruler.

"A holly jolly, very Merry Christmas, Bob!" Scrooge candidly bellowed, with an earnestness that could not be mistaken, as the cheerful businessman most eagerly clapped his main employee upon the back. "A merrier Christmas, Bob, my good fellow, than I have afforded you for many a year! I'll generously raise your miniscule salary, and I promise to assist your struggling family with their myriad obligations, and we will discuss your financial and personal affairs this very afternoon, over a Christmas bowl of smoking bishop; that is, if the pompous Archbishop of Canterbury is not available to be put on the hob. Ha, ha, ha! Now then, Bob! Make up our separate fires, and buy a second coal-scuttle before you dot another i, Bob Crot-shit! Er, I meant to politely say, Mr. Robert Crotchit!"

Over time, Scrooge's generosity was much better than his word. The benefactor did it all for everyone whom he had formerly neglected, and then infinitely more; and to Tiny Tim, who incidentally did NOT die, Ebenezer became a philanthropic second father.

The transformed, kind gentleman became as good a friend, as good a master, and as good a man as the good old city ever knew, or any other good old city, town, or borough in the good old world ever keenly recognized. Some pessimistic people laughed to see the radical alteration in his former brutal demeanor, but *his* own heart relentlessly laughed at *their* petulant criticisms, and that was quite enough expression for the elderly philanthropist's newly-discovered, gentle ego to contemplate.

Ebenezer Scrooge had no further spiritual intercourse with Spirits, but proceeded to live an insular-but-productive existence, and in that respect, his reformed conscience practiced his sworn adherence to the Total Abstinence Principle, ever afterwards. And it was always said of "the prosperous lunatic", cited by conscientious, local observers, that the "insane buffoon" knew how to keep Christmas in a very favorable manner, if any man alive ever possessed *that* specialized knowledge. May that be truly said of us, and of all of us! And so, as marvelous Tiny Tim philosophically observed and concluded," God Bless Us, Every One!"

About the Author

Jay Dubya is author John Wiessner's initials (J.W.) and also his pen name. John is a retired New Jersey public school English teacher, having taught the subject for thirty-four years. John lives in southern New Jersey with wife Joanne and the couple has three grown sons.

Jay Dubya has written other adult literature besides *Thirteen Sick Tasteless Classics, Part III. So Ya' Wanna' Be A Teacher*, *The Wholly Book of Genesis'*, *Black Leather and Blue Denim, A '50s Novel* and its sequel, *The Great Teen Fruit War, A 1960' Novel* are humorous literary endeavors. *Frat Brats, A '60s Novel* completes Jay Dubya's coming-of-age action/adventure trilogy. *Pieces of Eight, Pieces of Eight, Part II, Pieces of Eight Part III and Pieces of Eight, Part IV* are short story/novella collections featuring science fiction, paranormal and humorous plots and themes. *Nine New Novellas, NNN, Part II, NNN, Part III and NNN, Part IV* are other sci-fi/paranormal story collections. *Two Baker's Dozen* is another collection of short fiction works.

Ron Coyote, Man of La Mangia is adult humor and a satire/parody on Miguel Cervantes' *Don Quixote*, published in 1605. *The Wholly Book of Exodus* is adult satirical humor. *Thirteen Sick*

Tasteless Classics, *Thirteen Sick Tasteless Classics, Part II* and *TSTC, Part IV* are adult satirical rewrites of famous literary short fiction. Other satirical works are *Mauled Maimed Mangled Mutilated Mythology*, *Fractured Frazzled Folk Fables and Fairy Farces* and *FFFF & FF, Part II*.

John has also authored a trilogy of young adult fantasy novels, *Enchanta*, *Pot of Gold* and *Space Bugs, Earth Invasion*. *The Eighteen Story Gingerbread House* is a new collection of eighteen diverse children's stories.

Jay Dubya likes '50s rock and roll music, and he also enjoys pop' songs by the Beach Boys', Fleetwood Mac, the Eagles, the Rolling Stones, *ELO*, John Mellencamp and by John Fogerty. When not writing or listening to music, Jay Dubya likes watching *76ers* basketball and *Phillies* and *Yankees* television baseball games.

Author Biography

Born in Hammonton, NJ in 1942, John Wiessner had attended St. Joseph School up to and including Grade 5. After his family moved from Hammonton to Levittown, Pa in 1954, John attended St. Mark School in Bristol, Pa. for Grade 6, St. Michael the Archangel School in Levittown for Grades 7 and 8 and then Immaculate Conception School, Levittown, Pa. for Grade 9. Bishop Egan High School, Levittown PA. was John's educational base for Grades 10 and 11, and later in 1960, the aspiring author graduated from Edgewood Regional High, Tansboro, NJ. John then next attended Glassboro State College, where he was an announcer for the school's baseball games and also read the nightly news and sports over WGLS, GSC's radio station.

John Wiessner had been primarily an English teacher in the Hammonton Public School System for 34 years, specializing in the instruction of middle school language arts. Mr. Wiessner was quite active in the Hammonton Education Association, loyally serving in the capacities of Vice-President, then building representative, and finally, teachers' head negotiator for a period of 7 years. During his lengthy teaching career, John had been nominated into "Who's Who among American Teachers" three times. He also was quite active giving professional workshops at schools around South Jersey on the subjects of creative writing and the use of movie videos to motivate students to organize their classroom theme compositions.

In addition, John Wiessner was very active in community service, being a past President of the Hammonton Lions Club, where he also functioned for many years as the club's Tail-Twister, Vice-President and Liontamer. John had been named Hammonton Lion of the Year in 1979 and in 2009 received the prestigious Melvin Jones Fellow Award, the highest honor a Lion can receive.

John also was a successful businessman, starting with being a Philadelphia Bulletin newspaper delivery boy for two-years in the late 1950s in Levittown, Pennsylvania. After his family moved back to New Jersey in 1959, John worked at his grandparents and his parents' farm markets, Square Deal Farm (now Ron's Gardens in Hammonton) and Pete's Farm Market in Elm, respectively. He later managed his wife's parents' farm market, White Horse Farms in Elm for three summers.

Also in a business capacity, for 16 summers starting in 1967 John Wiessner had co-owned Dealers Choice Amusement Arcade on the Ocean City, Maryland boardwalk and also co-owned the New Horizon Tee-Shirt Store for eight summers (1973-

'81) on the Rehoboth Beach, Delaware boardwalk. In addition, "Jay Dubya" was a co-owner of Wheel and Deal Amusement Arcade, Missouri Avenue and Boardwalk, Atlantic City. And then, for 18 summers beginning in 1986, John had been the Field Manager in charge of crew-leaders for Atlantic Blueberry Company (the world's largest cultivated blueberry farm), both the Weymouth and Mays Landing Divisions.

After retiring from teaching in 1999, writing under the pen name Jay Dubya (his initials), John Wiessner became the author of 69 books in the genre Action/Adventure Novels, Sci-Fi/Paranormal Story Collections, Adult Satire, Young Adult Fantasy Novels and also Non-Fiction Books. His books exist in hardcover, in paperback and in popular Kindle and Nook e-book formats.

In January of 2022, John Wiessner (Jay Dubya) was nominated into Marquis Who's Who in America, and in April of that same year, was one of nine distinguished Who's Who in America members honored with receiving Lifetime Achievement Awards, all nine sharing a news article of recognition aappearing in the Wall Street Journal.

Google: Jay Dubya books